Sweet Myth-tery of Life

Robert Asprin

Sweet Myth-tery of Life

Robert Asprin

Cover and Interior Art by Phil Foglio
Edited by Elizabeth B. Bobbitt

THE
DONNING COMPANY
PUBLISHERS
20TH
ANNIVERSARY

The Donning Company/Publishers
184 Business Park Drive, Suite 106
Virginia Beach, VA 23462

Steve Mull, General Manager
Elizabeth B. Bobbitt, Editor
Mary Eliza Midgett, Designer

Library of Congress Cataloging in Publication Data:
Asprin, Robert.
Sweet myth-tery of life / by Robert L. Asprin :
cover and interior art by Phil Foglio.
p. cm. — (Myth adventure series)
ISBN 0-89865-858-6 — ISBN 0-89865-859-4 (limited edition)
1. Title. II. Title: Sweet mythtery of life. III. Series:
Asprin, Robert. Myth adventure series.
PS3551.S6S93 1994   93-47256
813'.54—dc20   CIP
Printed in the United States of America

This volume is dedicated to my friends and counselors who helped me break through a two-and-a-half-year writing block, including (but not restricted to):

> Mystia Deemer
> Todd and Mary Brantley
> Darlene Bolesney
> Randy Herbert
> Roger Zelasny
> The NO Quarter Sword Club

To the publishers and readers who have waited so patiently and loyally while I worked my way through this difficult period in my life, I feel the best way to express my thanks is to keep writing!

R. L. A.

Chapter One

*"Is it just me, or does it seem to you
I get more than my share of troubles?"*
—Job

"**A**nd so, to recap, the situation is this . . ."

I ticked the points off on my fingers, giving my audience a visual image to reinforce my words.

"First, Queen Hemlock wants me to be her consort. Second, she's given me a month to think it over before I reach my decision. Third . . ."

I tapped the appropriate finger for emphasis.

"If I decide *not* to marry her, she says she'll abdicate, naming *me* her successor and sticking me with the whole mess. Got that?"

Despite my concern over my predicament, I was nonetheless proud of my ability to address the problem head on, summarizing and analyzing it as I sought a solution. There was a time in the not too distant past when I simply would have lapsed into blind panic. If nothing else, my adventures over the years had done wonders for my confidence in my abilities to handle nearly any crisis.

"Gleep!" my audience responded.

Okay . . . so I wasn't all *that* confident.

While I knew I could muddle through most crises, the one situation I dreaded the most was making a fool of myself in front of my friends and colleagues. While they had always been unswerving in their loyalty and willingness to bail me out of whatever mess I blundered into, that didn't mean I was particularly eager to tax our friendships yet another time, even if it was just for advice. At the very least, I figured that when I *did* approach them, I should be as level-headed and mature about it as possible, rather than babbling hysterically about my woes. Consequently, I decided to rehearse my appeal in front of the one member of our crew I felt truly comfortable with . . . my pet dragon.

I've always maintained that Gleep is quite bright, despite the one-word vocabulary that gave him his name. According to my partner and mentor, Aahz, my pet's limited vocal range was merely a sign of his immaturity, and it would expand as he edged toward adulthood. Of course, realizing dragons live several centuries, the odds of my ever having a two-way conversation with Gleep were slim. At times like this, however, I actually appreciated having someone to talk to who could only listen . . . without helpful asides regarding my inability to walk across the street without landing myself and the crew in some kind of trouble.

"The trouble is," I continued, "what with all the problems and disasters I've had to cope with over the years, not to mention trying to be president of M.Y.T.H. Inc., I haven't had much time for a love life. like, none at all . . . and I *sure* haven't given any thought to getting *married!* I mean, I haven't ever really reached a decision on whether or not I want to get married *at all,* much less *when* or *to who.*"

Gleep cocked his head to one side, to all appearances hanging on my every word.

"Of course, I *do* know I'm not wild about the alternative. I had a chance to play king once . . . and that was *twice* too often, thank you. It was bad enough when I was just being a stand-in for Roderick, but the idea of trying to run the kingdom by myself, *as* myself, and forever, not just for a few days, well, that's flat out terrifying. The question is, is it more or less terrifying than the idea of being married to Queen Hemlock?"

My pet responded to my dilemma by vigorously chewing at an itch on his foot.

"Thanks a lot, Gleep old boy," I said, smiling wryly despite my ill humor. While I obviously hadn't really expected any glowing words of advice from my dragon, I had at least thought my problems were serious enough to hold his attention. "I might as well be talking to Aahz. At least *he* looks at me while he's chewing me out."

Still smiling, I picked up the goblet of wine I had brought with me for moral support and started to take a sip.

"Oh, Aahz isn't so bad."

For a startled moment, I thought Gleep had answered me. Then I realized the voice had come from behind me, not from my pet. A quick glance over my shoulder confirmed my worse fears. My partner, green scales, pointed teeth and all, was leaning against the wall not ten feet from where I stood, and had apparently been listening to my whole oration.

"Hi, Aahz," I said, covering my embarrassment with a forced smile. "I didn't hear you come in. Sorry about that last comment, but I've been a little . . ."

"Don't worry about it, Skeeve," he interrupted with a wave of dismissal. "If that's the worse you've had to say about me over the years, I figure we've been doing pretty well. I *do* lean on you kinda hard from time to time. I guess that's gotten to be *my* way of dealing with stress."

Aahz seemed calm enough . . . in fact, he seemed to be *suspiciously* calm. While I wasn't wild about his shouting at me, at least it was consistent. This new display of reasonability was making me uneasy . . . rather like suddenly noticing the sun just rose in the west.

"So . . . what are you doing here, partner?" I said, trying to sound casual.

"I was looking for you. It occurred to me that you might need a sympathetic ear while you figured out what to do next."

Again, a small warning gong went off in the back of my

mind. Of all the phrases that might occur to me to describe Aahz's interaction with me in the past, "a sympathetic ear" wasn't one of them.

"How did you know where I was?"

I was dodging the issue, but genuinely curious as to how Aahz found me. I had taken great pains to slip down to the Royal Stables unnoticed.

"It wasn't hard," Aahz said, flashing a grin as he jerked his thumb at the door. "You've got quite a crowd hanging around outside."

"I do?"

"Sure. Pookie may be a bit mouthy for my taste, but she knows her stuff as a bodyguard. I think she's been tailing you from the time you left your room."

Pookie was the new bodyguard I had acquired during my recent trip to Perv . . . before I knew she was Aahz's cousin.

"That's funny," I scowled. "I never saw her."

"Hey, I said she was good," my partner winked. "Just because she respects your privacy and stays out of sight doesn't mean she's going to let you wander around unescorted. Anyway, I guess Guido spotted her and decided to tag along . . . he's been following her around like a puppy ever since they met . . . and, of course, that meant Nunzio had to come, too, and . . . Well, the end result is you've got all three of your bodyguards posted outside the door to see to it that you aren't disturbed."

Terrific. I start out looking for a little privacy and end up leading a parade.

"So, what do you think, Aahz?" I said.

I knew I was going to get his opinion sooner or later, and figured I might as well ask outright and get it over with.

"About what?"

"About my problem," I clarified.

"What problem?"

"Sorry. I thought you had been listening when I explained it to Gleep. I'm talking about the whole situation with Queen Hemlock."

"I know," my partner said. "And I repeat, what problem?"

"*What problem?*" I was starting to lose it a little, which is not an unusual result of talking to Aahz. *"Don't you think . . ."*

"Hold on a second, partner," Aahz said, holding up his hand. "Do you remember the situation when we first met?"

"Sure."

"Let me refresh you memory, anyway. Your old mentor, Garkin, had just been killed, and there was every chance you were next on the hit list. Right?"

"Right. But . . ."

"Now *that* was a problem," He continued as if I hadn't spoken. "Just like it was a problem when you had to stop Big Julie's army with a handful of misfits . . . realizing that, if you were successful, Grimble was threatening to have you killed or worse when you returned to the palace."

"I remember."

"And when you decided to try to clear me of that murder rap over on Limbo, a dimension which just happens to be filled with vampires and werewolves, I'd say that was a problem, too."

"I don't see what . . ."

"Now, in direct contrast, let's examine the *current* situation. As I understand it, you're in danger of getting married to the Queen, which, I believe, includes having free run of the kingdom's treasury. The other option is that you decide not to marry her, whereupon she abdicates to you . . . leaving you again with a free hand on the treasury, only without the Queen." He showed me his impressive array of teeth. "I repeat, what problem?"

Not for the first time, it occurred to me that my partner had a tendency to appraise the pluses and minuses of any situation by the simple technique of reducing everything to monetary terms and scrutinizing the bottom line.

"The problem is," I said tersely, "that in order to *get* that access to the treasury, I have to get married or become king. Frankly, I'm not sure I'm wild about either option."

"Compared to what you've been through in the past to scrape together a few coins, it's not bad," Aahz shrugged. "Face it, Skeeve. Making a bundle usually involves something unpleasant. Nobody . . . and I mean *nobody* . . . is going to fork over hard cash for your having a good time."

Of course, those "few coins" we had scraped together over the past years added up to enough to make even a Pervish banker sit up and take notice, but I knew the futility of trying to convince Aahz that there was *ever* such a thing as enough money.

"Maybe I could just write about having dubious adventures instead of actually doing anything," I muttered. "That always sounded to me like a pretty cushy job to cash in on the good life."

"You think so? Well, let me educate you to the harsh realities of the universe, partner. It's one thing to practice a skill or a hobby when you feel like it, but whether it's writing, singing, or playing baseball, when you've *got* to do something whether you're up for it or not, *it's work!*"

I could see this conversation was going nowhere. Aahz simply wasn't going to see my point of view, so I decided to play dirty. I switched to *his* point of view.

"Maybe I'd be more enthusiastic," I said, carefully, "if the kingdom's finances weren't at rock bottom. Doing something unpleasant to acquire a stack of debts doesn't strike me as all that great a deal."

Okay. It was hitting below the belt. But that just happens to be where Pervects such as Aahz are the most sensitive . . . which is to say where they keep their wallets.

"You've got a point there," my partner said thoughtfully, wavering for the first time in the conversation. "Still, you managed to finagle a whole month before you have to make a decision. I figure in that time we should be able to get a pretty good fix on what the *real* financial situation around here is . . . *and* if it can be turned around."

"There's just one problem with that," I pointed out. "I know even less about money than I know about magik."

"Just off hand, I'd say you were doing pretty well in both departments."

I caught the edge in my partner's voice, and realized that he was on the brink of taking my comment personally . . . which is not surprising as he was the one who taught me nearly everything I know about magik *and* money.

"Oh, I'm okay when it comes to personal finances and contract negotiations . . . more than okay, in fact . . . and I have you to thank for that." I said hastily. "What we're looking at now, though, is *high* finance . . . as in trying to manage the funds for a whole kingdom! I don't think *that* was covered in my lessons, or if it was, it went over my head."

"Okay. That's a valid concern," Aahz conceded. "Still, it's probably the same thing you've been doing for M.Y.T.H. Inc., but on a larger scale."

"That's fine, except Bunny's been doing most of the heavy financial work for M.Y.T.H. Inc.," I grimaced. "I only wish she were here now."

"She is," Aahz exclaimed, clicking his fingers. "*That's* the other reason I was looking for you."

"Really? Where is she?"

"Waiting in your room. I wasn't sure what kind of sleeping arrangements you wanted set up."

One of the changes from my previous stay at the palace was that instead of sharing a room with Aahz, I had a room of my own. It's a tribute to how worried I was, however, that the implications of what he said went right over my head.

"Same as always," I said. "See if we can find a room for her that's at least in the same wing of the palace as ours, though."

"If you say so," Aahz shrugged. "Anyway, we'd better get going. She seemed real anxious to see you."

I only listened to this last with half an ear, as something else had momentarily caught my attention.

I had turned away from Aahz to give Gleep one last pat before we left, and for the barest fraction of a second saw something I had never noticed before. He was listening to us!

Now, as I noted earlier, I've always maintained that Gleep was bright, but as I turned, I had a fleeting impression of intelligence in his expression. To clarify, there *is* a difference between "bright" and "intelligent." "Bright," as I'd always applied it to my pet, means that he is alert and quick to learn. "Intelligent," on the

13

other hand, goes beyond "monkey see, monkey do" tricks, all the way to "independent thought."

Gleep's expression as I turned was one of thoughtful concentration, if not calculation. Then he saw me looking at him and the look disappeared, to be replaced with his more familiar expression of eager friendliness.

For some reason, this gave me a turn. Perhaps it was because I found myself remembering reports from the team about their efforts to disrupt the kingdom in my absence. Specifically, I was recalling the claim that Gleep had nearly killed Tananda . . . something I had dismissed at the time as being an accident that was being blown out of proportion in their effort to impress me with the difficulties of their assignment. Now, however, as I stared at my pet, I began to wonder if I should have paid closer attention to what they were saying. Then again, maybe it had just been the light playing tricks on me. Gleep certainly looked innocent enough now.

"Com'on, partner," Aahz repeated testily. "You can play with your dragon some other time. I still think we should try to sell that stupid beast off before he eats his way through our bankroll. He really doesn't add anything to our operation . . . except food bills."

Because I was already watching, I caught it this time. For the briefest moment Gleep's eyes narrowed as he glanced at Aahz, and an almost unnoticeable trickle of smoke escaped from one nostril. Then he went back to looking dopey and innocent.

"Gleep's a friend of mine now, Aahz," I said carefully, not taking my eyes off my pet. "Just like you and the rest of the crew are. I wouldn't want to lose *any* of you."

My dragon seemed to take no notice of my words, craning his neck to look around the stable. Now, however, it seemed to me his innocence was exaggerated . . . that he was deliberately avoiding looking me in the eye.

"If you say so," Aahz shrugged, heading for the door. "In the meantime, let's go see Bunny before she explodes."

I hesitated a moment longer, then followed him out of the stables.

Chapter Two

"It's good to see you, too."
H. Livingston, M.D.

As Aahz had predicted, my three bodyguards were waiting for me outside the stables. They seemed to be arguing about something, but broke off their discussion and started looking vigilant as soon as I appeared.

Now, you may think it would be kind of fun to have your own bodyguards. If so, you've never actually had one.

What it really means is that you give up any notion that your life is your own. Privacy becomes a vague memory you have to work at recalling, as "sharing" becomes the norm . . . starting with the food on your plate and ending with going to the john. ("Geez, Boss! You know how many guys got whacked because someone was hiding in the can? Just pretend we ain't here.") Then, too, there's the constant, disquieting reminder that, however swell a fellow **you** may think you are, there are people out there waiting for a chance to bring your career to a premature conclusion. I had to keep telling myself that this latter point didn't apply to me, that Don Bruce had insisted on assigning me Guido and Nunzio more as status symbols than anything else. I had hired Pookie on my own, though, after getting

15

jumped during my recent trip to Perv, so I couldn't entirely discount the fact that bodyguards were occasionally necessary and not just an inconvenient decoration.

"Got a minute, Skeeve?" Pookie said, stepping forward.

"Well, I was on my way to say hello to Bunny . . ."

"Fine. We can talk as we walk."

She fell in step beside me, and Aahz graciously fell back to walk with my other two bodyguards.

"What it is," Pookie said, without preamble, "is I'm thinking of cashing in and heading back to Perv."

"Really? Why."

She gave a small shrug.

"I can't see as how I'm really needed," she said. "When I suggested I tag along, we thought you were coming back to a small war. The way I see it now, it seems like the crew you've already got can handle things."

As she spoke, I snuck a glance back at Guido. He was trudging along, his posture notably more hang dog than usual. It was clear both that he was infatuated with Pookie, and that he wasn't wild about the idea of her moving on.

"Umm . . . Actually, I'd prefer it if you stuck around for a while, Pookie," I said. "At least, until I've made up my mind what to do about this situation with Queen Hemlock. She's been known to be a bit nasty when things don't go her way."

"Suit yourself," Pookie said, giving another shrug. "I just wanted to give you an easy out if you were looking to trim the budget."

I gave a smile at that.

"Just because we're going to be working on the kingdom's finances doesn't mean there's anything wrong with our treasury. You should know your cousin well enough to have faith in his money managing."

"I know Aahz, all right," she said, shooting a dark look at that individual, "enough to know that before he'd part with money unnecessarily, he'd cut off his arm . . . or, more likely, someone else's."

16

"He's mellowed a bit over the last few years," I smiled, "but I know what you mean. If it makes you feel any better, though, I hired you, so I figure you're reporting directly to me and not to him."

Pookie cocked an eyebrow at me.

"If that wasn't the case," she said, "I wouldn't have come along in the first place."

I could have let it go, but my curiosity was aroused.

"What's the problem between you two, anyway? More specifically, what's your problem with Aahz? He has nothing but the highest praise for you and your work."

Pookie's features hardened, and she broke eye contact to stare straight ahead.

"That's between him and me," she said stonily.

Her attitude puzzled me, but I knew better than to pursue the subject further.

"Oh. Well . . . anyway, I'd like you to stick around if that's okay."

"No problem from my end," she said. "Just one thing . . . to ease my mind. Could we adjust my pay scale? The prices you've been paying are my premium rates for short term work. For long term employment, I can give you a discount."

"How much?" I said quickly. As I noted before, Aahz had taught me most of what I know about money, and I had picked up some of his reflexes along the way.

"Why don't we knock it down to the same rate as you're paying those two," she said, jerking a thumb at Guido and Nunzio. "If nothing else, it might avoid some hard feelings between us professionally."

"Umm . . . fine."

I didn't have the heart to tell her that Guido and Nunzio were actually earning more than her premium rates. Realizing she was not only from the same dimension, but the same family as Aahz, I wasn't sure how she'd take the news. With everything else on my mind, I decided to sort it out at a later date . . . like, payday.

"Well, that takes care of me," Pookie said. "Any general orders for us?"

17

"Yes. Tell Nunzio I'd like to have a word with him."

One thing about living in a palace is that it takes a long time to walk from anywhere to anywhere, giving us lots of time to have conferences on the way to other conferences. Hey, I didn't say that it was a nice thing about living in a palace . . . just a thing.

"So what's the word, Boss?" Nunzio said, falling in step at my side.

"Is she stayin' or goin'?"

"What? Oh. Staying, I guess."

"Whew! That's a relief!" he said, rolling his eyes briefly. "I'll tell you, I don't think Guido would be livable if she left right now . . . know what I mean?"

"Uh huh," I said, glancing back at his cousin . . . who, judging by the grin on his face, had already heard the news. "He seems quite taken with her."

"You don't know the half of it," Nunzio grimaced. "So, what did you want to talk to me about?"

"Well, you know how you've been saying that Gleep has been acting strange lately?"

"Yeah. So?" he said, his squeaky voice taking on a cautious note.

"I want you to try to spend more time with him. Talk to him . . . maybe take him out for some exercise."

"Me, Boss?"

"Sure. You get along with him better than anyone . . . except, maybe, me . . . and I'm going to be tied up with the kingdom's finances for a while. If there's anything wrong with Gleep, I want to find out about it before anyone else gets hurt."

"If you say so."

I couldn't help but notice an extreme lack of enthusiasm in his voice.

"Yes. I say so," I repeated firmly. "It's important to me, Nunzio, and I can't think of anyone I'd trust more check things out for me."

"Okay, Boss," he said, thawing a little. "I'll get right on it."

I wanted to give him a bit more encouragement, but just then we arrived at the door to my quarters.

"I'll wait out here, Boss, and make sure nobody else comes in for a while," Nunzio said with a faint smile as he stepped back.

This surprised me a little, as the crew usually followed me into my room without missing a step or a syllable of conversation. Then I noticed that the others of our group had also halted short of the door and were watching me with a smile.

I couldn't figure what was going on. I mean, so Bunny was waiting inside. So what? It was just Bunny.

Nevertheless I took my cue, nodding at them vaguely as I opened the door.

"SKEEVE!!"

I barely turned around from shutting the door when Bunny charged across the room, slamming into me with a huge hug that took my breath away . . . literally.

"I was so worried about you!" she said, her voice muffled by my chest.

"Ahh . . . ack!"

That last comment was mine. Actually, it wasn't so much a comment as a noise I made while trying to force some air into my lungs. This proved easier said than done . . . and it wasn't all that easy to say!

"Why didn't you come by the office on your way back from Perv?" Bunny demanded, squeezing even harder and shaking me slightly. "I was going out of my mind, thinking about you all alone in that terrible dimension . . ."

By ignoring what she was saying and focusing my entire consciousness on moving, I managed to slowly force one hand . . . then an arm . . . inside her embrace. Summoning my fast fading strength, I levered my arm sideways, breaking her grip and allowing myself a desperately needed rush of air.

Okay. So it wasn't particularly affectionate, or even polite. It's just that I've picked up some annoying, selfish habits over the years . . . like breathing.

"What's the matter, Skeeve?" Bunny said in a concerned

voice, peering at me closely. "Are you all right?"

"UUUUH hah . . . UUUUH hah . . . ," I explained, realizing for the first time how sweet plain air could taste.

"I knew it!" she snarled. "Tananda kept saying you were all right . . . every time I asked she kept saying the same thing . . . that you were all right. The next time I see that little . . ."

"I'm . . . fine . . . Really, Bunny. I'm . . . . fine."

Still trying to get my lungs working on their own, I reached out a tentative finger and prodded her biceps.

"That was . . . quite a 'Hello,'" I said. "I never realized . . . you were so . . . strong."

"Oh, that." she shrugged. "I've been working out a little while you were gone . . . like every night. Not much else to do evenings. It's an easier way to stay in shape than dieting."

"Working out?"

My breathing was almost back to normal, but my head still felt a little woozy.

"Sure. You know, pumping iron?"

I had never realized that simple ironing could build up a woman's arms that much. I made a mental note to start sending our laundry out.

"I'm sorry I didn't think to check in with you," I said, returning to the original subject. "It's just that I assumed you were okay there at the office, and was in a hurry to see if the crew was okay."

"Oh, I know. It's just that . . ."

Suddenly she was hugging me again . . . gentler, this time.

"Don't be mad at me, Skeeve," she said softly from the depths of my chest. "I just get so worried about you sometimes."

I was surprised to realize she was trembling. I mean, it just wasn't that cold here in my room. Especially not huddled together the way we were.

"I'm not mad at you, Bunny," I said. "And there was nothing to worry about . . . really. Everything went fine on Perv."

"I heard that you nearly got killed in a fight," she countered, tightening her grip slightly. "And wasn't there some kind of trouble with the cops?"

That annoyed me a little. The only way she could have found out about the trouble I ran into on Perv would be from Tananda . . . except I hadn't told Tananda anything about it before she headed back to the Bazaar to relieve Bunny. That meant that either Aahz or Pookie was telling people about my escapades . . . and, to say the least, I wasn't wild about that.

"Where did you hear that?" I said casually.

"It's all over the Bazaar," Bunny explained, burrowing further into my chest. "Tananda said you were fine, but I had to see for myself after everything I heard."

Com'on, Bunny," I said soothingly, mentally apologizing to Aahz and Pookie. "You know how everything gets exaggerated at the Bazaar. You can see I'm fine."

She started to say something, then turned her head as sounds of an argument erupted through the closed door.

"What's that?"

"I don't know," I admitted. "Guido and Nunzio said they were going to keep everybody out for a while. Maybe someone . . ."

The door burst open, and Queen Hemlock stood framed in the entryway. Behind her my bodyguards stood, and as they caught my eye gave exaggerated shrugs. Apparently royalty was harder to stop than your average assassin . . . a thought that did little to cheer me realizing some of the rumors surrounding the current matriarch of Possiltum.

"There you are, Skeevie," the Queen exclaimed striding into my room. "I was looking all over for you when I saw those thugs of yours loitering about outside and . . . Who's this?"

"Your Majesty, this is Bunny. Bunny, this is Queen Hemlock."

"Your majesty," Bunny said, sinking into a deep bow.

It occurred to me that as worldly as she was in some ways, Bunny had never met a member of royalty before, and seemed to be quite awed by the experience.

Queen Hemlock, on the other hand, was not at all overawed by meeting another commoner.

"Why Skeeve! She's lovely!" she said, cupping Bunny's chin in her hand and raising her head to view her face. "I was starting to wonder a bit about you, what with that monstrous apprentice of yours, not to mention that lizard thing you brought back with you from wherever, but *this* . . . It's nice to know you *can* find a yummy morsel when you set your mind to it."

"Bunny's my administrative assistant," I said, a bit stiffly.

"Why of *course!*" the Queen smiled, giving me a broad wink. "Just like my young men are bodyguards . . . on the kingdom budget, anyway."

"Please, your majesty, don't misunderstand," Bunny said. "Skeeve and I are really just . . ."

"There there, my dear," Hemlock interrupted, taking Bunny by the hands and drawing her to her feet. "There's no need to worry about me being jealous. I wouldn't dream of interfering in Skeeve's personal life before or after we're married, any more than I'd expect him to interfere in mine. As long as he does the heir thing to keep the rabble happy, It doesn't really matter to me what he does with the rest of his time."

I really didn't like the way this conversation was going, and hastened to change the subject.

"You said you were looking for me, your Majesty?"

"Oh yes," the Queen said, releasing her hold on Bunny's hands. "I wanted to tell you that Grimble was waiting to see you at your earliest convenience. I told him that you'd be giving him a hand straightening out the kingdom's finances, and he's ready to give you whatever information or assistance you need.

Somehow, that didn't sound like the J. R. Grimble I knew, but I let it slide for the moment.

"Very well. We'll be along presently."

"Of course." the Queen smiled, winking at me again. "Well, I'll just be running along then."

As she reached the door, she paused to sweep Bunny once more with a lingering gaze. "Charming," she said. "You really are to be congratulated, Skeeve."

There was an uncomfortable silence after the Queen left.

Finally, I cleared my throat.

"I'm sorry about that, Bunny. I guess she just assumed . . ."

"*That's* the woman you're supposed to marry?" Bunny said as if I hadn't spoken."

"Well, it's what she wants, but I'm still thinking it over."

"And if somebody kills her, you'd feel you had to take over running the kingdom?"

"Uh . . . well, yes."

There was something in Bunny's voice I didn't like. I also found myself remembering that while she had never met royalty before, her uncle was none other than Don Bruce, the Mob's Fairy Godfather, and that she was used to an entirely different brand of power politics.

"I see," Bunny said thoughtfully, then she broke into her usual smile. "Well, I guess we'd better go and see Grimble and find out what kind of a mess we're really in."

"Okay. Sure," I said, glad that the crisis had passed . . . if only for the moment.

"Just one question, Skeeve."

"Yes, Bunny?"

"How do *you* feel about 'the heir thing' as her majesty so graciously put it?"

"I don't know," I admitted. "I guess I don't mind."

"You don't?"

"Not really. I just don't understand what having a haircut has to do with being a royal consort."

Chapter Three

"A good juggler can always find work."
L. Paccioli*

J. R. Grimble, Chancellor of the Exchequer for the kingdom of Possiltum, had changed little since I first met him. A little more paunch around the waist, perhaps, though his slender body could stand the extra weight and then some, and his hairline had definitely progressed from the "receding" to the "receded" category, but aside from that the years had left him virtually unmarked. Upon reflection, I decided it was his eyes that were so distinctive as to render his other features inconsequential. They were small and dark, and glittered with the fervent light of a greedy rodent . . . or of someone who spent far too many hours pouring over the tiny scribbled figures which noted the movement of other peoples' money.

"Lord Skeeve!" he exclaimed, seizing my hand and pumping it enthusiastically. "So good to have you back. And Aahz! Couldn't stay way, eh?" He gave a playful wink at my partner.

[*I'll give you this one . . . Luca Paccioli— inventor of double-entry accounting, "Father of Bookkeeping—R. L. A.]

"Just kidding. Glad to see you again, too."

"Have you been drinking, Grimble?" Aahz said bluntly.

In all honesty, I had been wondering the same thing myself, but had been at a loss as to how to ask the question diplomatically. Fortunately, my partner's characteristic tactlessness came to my rescue.

"Drinking?" the Chancellor blinked. "Why, no. Why do you ask?"

"You seem a lot more cheerful than normal, is all. As a matter of fact, I don't recall your ever being happy to see either of us before."

"Now now, let's let bygones be bygones, shall we? Though I'll admit we've had our differences in the past, we're going to be working together now . . . and frankly, gentlemen, I can't think of anyone I'd rather have in my corner during our current financial crisis. I never felt at liberty to admit it before, but I've always secretly admired your skills when it came to manipulating monies."

"Uh . . . thanks, Grimble," I said, still unsure of exactly how to take his new attitude.

"And who do we have here?"

He turned his attention to Bunny, devouring her with his eyes like a toad edging up on a moth.

I suddenly recalled that Aahz and I had first become embroiled in the workings of Possiltum after Grimble had picked Tananda up in a singles bar. It also occurred to me that I didn't like Grimble much.

"This is Bunny," I said. "She's my administrative assistant."

"Of course," Grimble shot me a sidelong, reptilian glance, then went back to leering at Bunny. "You always did have exquisite taste in ladies, Skeeve."

Still annoyed at Bunny's treatment by Queen Hemlock, I wasn't about to let the Chancellor get away with this.

"Grimble," I said, letting my voice take on a bit of an edge. "Watch my lips. I said she's my administrative assistant. Got it?"

"Yes. I . . . Quite."

The Chancellor seemed to pull in on himself a bit as he licked his lips nervously, but he rallied back gamely.

"Very well. Let me show you our expanded operation."

While Grimble might have been essentially unchanged, physically or morally, his facilities were another matter entirely. He had formerly worked alone in a tiny, cramped cubicle filled past capacity with stacks and piles of paper. The paper was still there, but that's about all that remained the same. Instead of the cubicle, it seemed he was now working out of a spacious, though still windowless, room . . . or, at least, a room that would have been spacious if he had it to himself.

Instead, however, there were over a dozen individuals crammed into the space, apparently preoccupied with their work, which seemed to entail nothing more than generating additional stacks of paper, all covered by columns and rows of numbers. They didn't look up as we came in, and Grimble made no effort to halt their work or make introductions, but I noticed that they all had the same fevered glint to their eyes that I had originally assumed to be unique to Grimble.

"It seems that the current financial crisis hasn't caused many cut-backs in your operation," Aahz said drily.

"Of course not," Grimble replied easily. "That's only to be expected."

"How's that?" I said.

"Well, Lord Skeeve," the Chancellor smiled, "you'll find that accountants are pretty much like vultures . . . we thrive when things are worse for other people. You see, when a kingdom or company is doing well, no one wants to be bothered with budgets, much less cost savings. As long as there's money in the coffers, they're happy. On the other hand, when the operation is on the skids, such as is currently the case with Possiltum, *then* everyone wants answers . . . or miracles . . . and it's up to us irritating bean-counters to provide them. More analysis means more man-hours, which in turn means a larger staff and expanded facilities."

"Charming," Aahz growled, but Grimble ignored him.

"So," he said, rubbing his hands together like a blow-fly, "what would you like to address first? Perhaps we could discuss our overall approach and strategy over lunch?"

"Umm . . ." I said intelligently.

The horrible truth was that, now that I was actually confronted by Grimble and his paper mountains, I didn't have the foggiest notion of how to proceed.

"Actually, Grimble," Bunny said stepping forward, "before we think about lunch, I'd like to see your Operating Plan for the current year, the calendarized version, as well as the P and L's and Financial Statements for the last few months . . . oh yes, and your Cash Flow Analysis, both the projections and the actuals, if you don't mind."

The Chancellor blanched slightly and swallowed hard.

"Certainly. I . . . of course," he said, giving Bunny a look which was notably more respectful than his earlier attentions. "I'll get those for you right now."

He scuttled off to confer with a couple of his underlings, all the while glancing nervously back at our little group.

I caught Aahz's eye and raised an eyebrow, which he responded to with a grimace and a shrug. It was nice to know my partner was as much in the dark as I was regarding Bunny's requests.

"Here we are," Grimble said, returning with a fistful of paper which he passed to Bunny. "I'll have the Cash Flow for you in a moment, but you can get started with these."

Bunny grunted something non-committal, and began leafing through the sheets, pausing to scrutinize each page intently. More for show than anything, I eased over to where I could look over her shoulder. In no time flat, my keen eye could tell without a doubt that the pages were filled with rows and columns of numbers. Terrific.

"Um . . . I do have some spread sheets to support some of those figures if you'd like to see them," Grimble supplied uneasily.

Bunny paused in her examinations to favor him with a dark glance.

"Maybe later," she said. "I mean, you *do* know the origin of spread sheets, don't you?"

"Umm . . ." the Chancellor hedged.

"They were named after the skins used by trappers," Bunny continued with a faint smile. "You know, the things they dragged after them to hide their tracks?"

For a moment Grimble stared at her, bewildered, then he gave a sudden bark of laughter, slapping her playfully on the shoulder.

"That's good!" he exclaimed. "I'll have to remember that one."

I glanced at Aahz

"Accountant humor, I guess," he said with a grimace. "Incomprehensible to mere mortals. You know, like 'We'll make it up on volume' jokes?"

"Now *that's* not funny," Grimble corrected with mock severity. "We've had that line dumped on us all too often . . . in complete sincerity. Right Bunny?"

I couldn't help but notice that he was now treating Bunny with the deference of a colleague. Apparently her joke, however nonsensical it had been to me, had convinced the Chancellor that she was more than my arm ornament.

"Too true," my 'assistant' said. "But seriously, Grimble, getting back to the problem at hand, we're going to need complete, non-camouflaged figures if we're going to get the kingdom's finances back on course. I know the tradition is to pretty things up with charts and studies of historic trends, but since we'll be working with insiders only, just this once let's try it with hard, cold data."

It sounded like a reasonable request to me, but the Chancellor seemed to think it was a radical proposal . . . and not a particularly wise one, at that.

"I don't know, Bunny," he said, shooting a look at Aahz and me one normally reserves for spies and traitors. "I mean, you know how it is. Even though we usually get cast as the villains of bureaucracy, we don't have any *real* power to implement change. All we do is make recommendations to those who *can* change things. If we don't sugarcoat our recommendations, or slant them so they're in line with what the movers and shakers wanted to hear all along, or clutter them up until the Gods themselves can't understand what we're really saying, then there's a risk that *we* end up being what gets changed."

"Nobody *really* wants to hear the truth, eh?" Aahz said, sympathetically. "I suppose that's typical. I think you'll find it's different this time around, Grimble. If nothing else, Skeeve here has full power to implement whatever changes he thinks are necessary to bring things in line."

"That's right," I said, glad to finally be able to contribute to the proceedings. "One of the things I think we should do as soon as possible is cut back on the size of the army . . . say, maybe, by one-half?"

Knowing the Chancellor's long-time feud with military spending, I thought he'd leap at this suggestion, but to my surprise, he shook his head.

"Can't do it," he said. "It would cause a depression."

"I don't care it they're happy or not!" Aahz snarled. "Let's get 'em off the payroll. The Queen's agreed to stop her expansionist policies, so there's no reason we should keep paying for an army this size."

Grimble gave my partner a look like he was something unpleasant on the bottom of his shoe.

"I was referring to an economic depression," he said tersely. "If we dump that many ex-soldiers on the job market at the same time we're cutting back on military spending, it would create massive unemployment. Broke, hungry people, particularly those with prior military training, have a nasty tendency to revolt against those in power . . . which, in this case, happens to be us. I think you'll agree, therefore, that, in the long run, huge cutbacks in the military force is n*ot* the wisest course to follow."

I was rapidly developing a greater respect for Grimble. Obviously there was more to this bean-counting game than I had ever imagined.

"We might, however, achieve some savings through attrition," the Chancellor continued.

"Attrition?" I said. I had decided that, if I was going to be any help at all in this effort, it was time I admitted my ignorance and started learning some of the basic vocabulary.

"In this case, Lord Skeeve," Grimble explained with surprising patience, "the term refers to cutting manpower by not rehiring as people terminate at the normal rate . . . or, for the army, that we stop adding new recruits to replace those whose term of enlistment is up. It will still cut the size of the army, but at a slower rate more easily absorbed by the civilian work force."

"Can we afford to do it slowly?" Aahz said, seemingly unfazed by his earlier rebuke. "I was under the impression the kingdom was in dire straits financially."

"I believe I had heard some rumor that we might be raising our tax rate?" The Chancellor made the statement a question as he looked at me pointedly.

"I'm not sure that will do any good," Bunny said from where she was reviewing the figures Grimble had passed her.

"Excuse me?" the Chancellor frowned.

"Well, from what I'm seeing here, the big problem isn't income, it's collections," she said, tapping one of the sheets she was holding.

Grimble sighed, seeming to deflate slightly.

"I'll admit that's one of our weak suits," he said, "But . . ."

"Whoa! Time out!" I interrupted. "Could someone provide a translation?"

"What I'm saying is that the kingdom actually has a fair amount of money," Bunny said, "but it's all on paper. That is, people owe us a lot on back taxes, but it isn't being collected. If we could make some inroads into converting these receivables . . . that's debts owed to us . . . into cash, which we can spend, the kingdom would be in pretty good shape. Not stellar, mind you, but enough to ease the current crisis."

"The problem is," Grimble said, picking up the thread of her oration, "the citizens are *extremely* un-cooperative when it comes to taxes. They fight us every inch of the way in admitting how much they owe, and when it comes to actually *paying* their tax bill . . . well, the variety of excuses they invent would be amusing, if we weren't going bankrupt waiting for them to settle their accounts."

"I can't argue with them there," Aahz smirked.

"It's the duty of every citizen to pay their far share of the cost of running the kingdom through taxes," the Chancellor said testily.

"And it's the right of every individual to pay the lowest possible amount of taxes they can justify legally," my partner shot back.

For a moment, it sounded like old times, with Aahz and Grimble going head to head. Unfortunately, this time, we all had bigger fish to fry.

"Check me on this," I said, holding up a hand to silence them. "What if we see if we can kill two birds with one stone?"

"How's that?" Grimble frowned.

"Well, first, we implement your suggestion of reducing the army by attrition . . . maybe hurrying it along a little by offering shortened enlistments for anyone who wanted out early . . ."

"That might help," the Chancellor nodded, "but I don't see . . ."

"*And,*" I continued quickly, "convert a portion of those remaining in the service into tax collectors. That way they can be helping to raise the cash necessary to cover their own pay."

Grimble and Bunny looked at each other.

"That might work," Grimble said, thoughtfully.

"It can't do much worse than the system that's already in place," Bunny nodded.

"Tell you what," I said loftily. "Kick it around between the two of you and maybe rough out a plan for implementing it. Aahz and I will go discuss it with the Queen."

Actually, I had no intention of visiting Hemlock just now, but I figured it was as good a time as any to escape from this meeting . . . while I had at least a small victory to my credit.

Chapter Four

"I'm getting paid how *much?"*
M. Jordan

The next several days were relatively uneventful. In fact, they seemed so much alike that I tended to lose track of which day was which.

If this sounds like I was more than a little bored, I was. After years of adventuring and narrow escapes, I found the day to day routine of regular work to be pretty bland. Of course, the fact that I didn't know what I was doing contributed greatly to my mood.

I mean, within my own areas of specialization . . . such as running from angry mobs or trying to finagle a better deal from a client . . . I was ready to admit that I was as good or better than anyone. At things like budgets, operating plans, and cash flows, however, I was totally out of my depth.

It was more than a little spooky when I realized that, even though I didn't know what I was doing, the recommendations I was making or approving, like converting part of the army into tax collectors, were becoming law nearly as fast as I spoke. Still, it had been impressed on me that we had to do *something* to save the kingdom's finances, so I repeatedly crossed my fingers under the table and went with whatever seemed to be the best idea at the time.

Before I get too caught up in complaining about my situation, however, let me pause to give credit where credit is due. As bad as things were, I would have been totally lost without Bunny.

Though I didn't plan it that way, my administrative assistant ended up doing double duty. First, she would spend long hours going over numbers and plans with Grimble in their high speed, abbreviated jargon while I sat there nodding with a vacant look on my face, then an equal or greater amount of time with me later patiently trying to explain what had been decided. As mind numbing as it was, I found it preferable to my alternate pastime, which was trying to figure out what to do about Queen Hemlock's marriage offer.

Every so often, however, something would pop up that I felt I DID know something about. While it would usually turn out in the long run that I was (badly) mistaken, it would provide a break from the normal complacency. Of course, I wasn't that wild about being shown to be *specifically* stupid as well as generally ignorant, but it was a change of pace.

One conversation in particular springs to mind when I think back on those sessions.

"Wait a minute, Bunny. What was that last figure again?"

"What?" she said, glancing up from the piece of paper she was reciting from. "Oh, that was *your* budget."

"My budget for what?"

"For your portion of the financial operation, of course. It covers salaries and operating expense."

"Whoa! Stop the music!" I said, holding up my hand. "I officially retired as Court Magician. How did I end up back on the payroll?"

"Grimble put you back on the same day you came back from Perv," Bunny said patiently. "But that has nothing to do with this. This is your budget for your *financial* consulting. Your magical fees are in a whole separate section."

"But that's ridiculous!"

"Oh Skeeve," she grimaced, rolling her eyes slightly. "I've explained all this to you before. We *have* to keep the budgets for different kingdom operations on separate records to be able to track their performance accurately. Just like we have to keep the types of expenses within each operation in separate accounts. Otherwise . . . "

"No, I didn't mean that it was ridiculous to keep them in separate sections," I clarified hastily, before she could get settled into yet another accounting lesson. "I meant the budget itself was ridiculous."

For some reason, this seemed to get Bunny even more upset rather than calming her down.

"Look, Skeeve," she said stiffly. "I know you don't understand everything Grimble and I are doing, but believe me, I don't just make these numbers up. That figure for your budget is a reasonable projection, based on estimated expenses and current pay scales . . . even Grimble says it's acceptable and has approved it. Realizing that, I'd be *very* curious to hear the exact basis by which you're saying it's ridiculous."

"You don't understand, Bunny," I said, shaking my head. "I'm not saying the number is ridiculous or inaccurate. What I mean is that it shouldn't be there at all."

"What do you mean?"

I was starting to feel like we were speaking in different languages, but pressed on bravely.

"Com'on, Bunny. All this work is supposed to be *saving* money for the kingdom. You know, turning the finances around?"

"Yes, yes," Bunny nodded. "So what's your point?"

"So how does it help things to charge them *anything* for our services, much less an outrageous rate like *this*. For that matter, I don't hink I should charge them for my magical services, either, all things considered."

"Um, Partner?" Aahz said, uncoiling from his customary seat in the corner. If anything, I think he was even more bored by these sessions than I was. "Can I talk to you for a minute? Before this conversation goes any further?"

I *knew* what that meant. Aahz is notorious when it comes to pushing our rates higher, operating under the basic principle that earning less than possible is the same as losing money. As soon as I started talking about not only reducing our fees, but eliminating them completely, it was only to be expected that Aahz would jump into the fray. I mean talk about money in general, and about our money specifically, would bring Aahz out of a coma.

This time, however, I wasn't about to go along with him.

"Forget it, Aahz," I said, waving him off. "I'm not going to back off on this one."

"But **Partner**," he said menacingly, reaching out his hand casually for my shoulder.

"I said 'No!'" I insisted, ducking out of his reach. I've tried to argue with him before when he has gotten a death grip on my shoulder, and was not about to give him that advantage again. "*This* time I know I'm right."

"*What's right about working for FREE?*" he snarled, abandoning all subtlety. "*Haven't I taught you ANYTHING in all these years?*"

"**You've taught me a lot!!**" I shot back at him. "And I've gone along with a lot . . . and it usually turned out for the best.

But there's one thing we've never done, Aahz, for all our fina-gling and scrambling. To the best of my knowledge, *we've never gouged money out of someone who couldn't afford it.* Have we?"

"Well, no. But . . ."

"If we can beat the Deveels or the Mob out of some extra money, well and good," I continued. "They have lots of money, and got most of it swindling other people. But with Possiltum we're talking about a kingdom that's on the ropes financially. How can we say we're here to help them when at the same time we're kicking them in the head with inflated fees?"

Aahz didn't answer at once, and after a moment, he dropped his eyes.

"But Grimble's already approved it," he said finally, in a voice that was almost plaintive.

I couldn't believe it! I had actually won an argument with Aahz over money! Fortunately, I had the presence of mind to be magnanimous in my victory.

"Then I'm sure he'll approve of cutting the expense even more," I said, putting my hand on Aahz's shoulder for a change. "Aside from that, it's just a clerical adjustment. Right, Bunny?"

"No."

She said it softly, but there was no mistaking her answer. So much for my victory.

"But Bunny . . ." I began desperately, but she cut me off.

"I said 'No' and I meant it, Skeeve," she said. "Really, Aahz. I'm surprised you've let this go on for as long as it has. There are greater principles at stake here than basic greed!"

Aahz started to open his mouth, then closed it without speaking. It's probably the only time I've seen Aahz agree, even by silence, that there *existed* any higher principles than greed. Still, Bunny was arguing his side of the fight, so he let it ride.

"Your heart may be in the right place, Skeeve," she said, turning back to me, "but there are factors here you're overlook-ing or don't understand."

"So explain them to me," I said, a little miffed, but nonethe-less willing to learn.

Bunny pursed her lips for a moment, apparently organizing her thoughts.

"All right," she said, "let's take it from the beginning. As I understand it, we're supposed to be helping the kingdom get out of it's current financial crisis. What Grimble and I have been doing, aside from recommending emergency expense cuts, is to come up with a reasonable budget and operating plan to get things back on an even keel. The emphasis here is on *'reasonable.'* The bottom line is that it is **not** reasonable to expect anyone . . . you, me, or Grimble . . . to provide such a crucial service for nothing. **Nobody** works for free. The army doesn't, the farmers don't, and there's no reason we should."

"But because of that very crisis, the kingdom *can't* afford to pay us!" I protested.

"Nonsense," Bunny snapped. "First of all, remember that the Queen got the kingdom into this mess all by herself by pouring too much money into the army. We're not the problem. We're the imported experts who are supposed to get them out of the hole they dug for themselves."

"Second," she continued before I could interrupt, "as you can see from the sheets I'm showing you, we *can* save enough in expenses and generate sufficient revenues from taxes to pay our own fees. That's part of the job of a bean-counter . . . to show their employer how to afford to pay themselves. Not many professions do that!"

What she was saying made sense, but I was still unconvinced.

"Well, at the very least can't we cut our fees a bit?" I said. "There's no real reason for us to charge as much as you have us down for."

"Skeeve, Skeeve, Skeeve," Bunny said, shaking her head. "I told you I didn't just make up these numbers. I know you're used to negotiating deals on what the client will bear, but in a budget like this, the pay scale is almost dictated. It's set by what others are getting paid. Anything else is so illogical, it would upset the whole system."

I glanced at Aahz, but he had his eyes fixed on Bunny, hanging on her every word.

"Okay. Let's take it from the top," I said. "Explain it to me in babytalk, Bunny. Just how are these pay scales fixed?"

She pursed her lips for a moment while organizing her thoughts.

"Well, to start with, you have to understand that the pay scale for any job is influenced heavily by supply and demand." she began. "Top dollar jobs usually fall into one of three catagories. First, is if the job is particularly unpleasant or dangerous . . . then, you have to pay extra just to get someone to be willing to do it. Second are the jobs where a particular skill or talent is called for. Entertainers and athletes fall into this category, but so do jobs that require a high degree of training, like doctors."

"And magicians!" my partner chimed in.

"Bear with me, Aahz," Bunny said, holding up a restraining hand to him. "Now, the third category for high pay are those who have a high degree of responsibility . . . whose decisions involve a lot of money and/or affect a lot of people. If a worker in a corporation makes a mistake, it means a day's or a week's work may have to be redone . . . or, perhaps, a client is lost. The president of the same corporation may only make three or four decisions a year, but those decisions may be to open or close six plants or to begin or discontinue an entire line of products. If *that* person makes a mistake, it could put hundreds or thousands of people out of work. Responsibility of that level is frightening and wearing, and the person willing to hold the bag deserves a higher degree of compensation. With me so far?"

"It makes sense . . . so far," I nodded.

"Moving along then, within each profession, there's a pecking order with the best or most experienced getting the highest rates, while the newer, lower workers settle for starting wages. Popular entertainers earn more than relative unknowns who are still building a following. Supervisors and managers get more than those reporting to them, since they have to have both the necessary skills of the job *plus* the responsibility of organizing and overseeing others. This is the natural order of a job force, and it provides incentive for new workers to stick with a job and to try to move up in the order. Got it?"

"That's only logical," I agreed.

"Then you understand why I have you down in the budget for the rather substantial figure you've been protesting," she concluded triumphantly.

"I do?" I blinked.

I thought I had been following her fine, step by step. Somewhere along the way, however, I seemed to have missed something.

"Don't you see, Skeeve?" she pressed. "The services you're providing for Possiltum fall into *all three* of the high pay requirements. The work is dangerous *and* unpleasant, it definitely requires special skills from you and your staff, and, since you're setting policy for an entire kingdom, the responsibility level is right up there with the best of them!"

I had never stopped to think about it in those terms, mostly to preserve my nerves and sanity, but she *did* have a point. She wasn't done, however.

"What's more," she continued, "you're darn near at the top of your profession *and* the pecking order. Remember, Grimble's reporting to *you* now, which makes your pay scale higher than his. What's more, you've been a hot magical property for some time now . . . not just here on Klah, but at the Bazaar on Deva which is pretty big league. Your Queen Hemlock has gotten the kingdom in a major mess, and if she's going to hire the best to bail her out, she's bloody well going to pay for it."

That last part had an unpleasant sound of vindictiveness to it, but there was something that was bothering me even more.

"For the moment, let's say I agree with you . . . at least on the financial side," I said. "I still don't see how I can draw pay as a financial consultant *and* a court magician."

"Because you're doing both jobs," Bunny insisted.

" . . . But I'm not working magically right now," I shot back.

"Aren't you?" she challenged. "Come on, Skeeve. Are you trying to tell me that if some trouble arose that required a magikal solution, that you'd just stand by and ignore it?"

"Well, no. But . . ."

"No 'buts,'" Bunny interrupted. "You're in residence here, and ready to throw your full resources into any magikal assignment that arises . . . just like you're doing at the Bazaar. *They're* paying you a hefty percentage just to be on standby. If anything, you're giving Possiltum a break on what you're charging them. Make no mistake, though, you are doing the job. I'm just making sure they pay you for it. If they want a financial consultant and a court magician, then it's only fair that it shows in their budget and is part of the burden they have to raise money to pay."

She had me. It occurred to me, however, that if this conversation lasted much longer, she'd have me believing that black was white.

"I guess it's okay then," I said, shrugging my shoulders. "It still sounds high to me."

"It is," Bunny said, firmly. "You've got to remember though, Skeeve, that whole amount isn't just for you. It's M.Y.T.H. Inc. the kingdom is paying for. The fees have to cover the expense of your entire operation, including overhead and staff. It's not like you're taking the whole amount and putting it in your pocket."

I nodded casually, but my mind was racing. What Bunny had just said had given me an idea.

If nothing else, I had learned in these sessions that there was a big difference between a budget or operating plan and the actual money spent. Just because I was *allowed* to spend an astronomic figure didn't mean I was compelled to do it!

I quietly resolved to bring my sections in well under budget . . . even if it meant trimming my own staff a bit. I loved them all dearly, but as Bunny had just pointed out, part of my own job was to be highly responsible.

Chapter Five

"What you need is a collection agency."
D. Shultz

My session with Bunny had given me food for thought. Retreating to the relative privacy of my room, I took time to reflect on it over a goblet of wine.

Usually, I assigned people to work on various assignments for M.Y.T.H. Inc. on a basis of what I thought it would take to get the job done and who I thought would be best to handle it. That, and who was available.

As Bunny had pointed out, our prices were usually set on a basis of what the traffic would bear. I suppose I should have given more thought in the past to whether or not the income from a particular job covered the expense of the people involved, or if the work warranted the price, but operating the way we had been seemed to generate enough money to make ends meet . . . more than enough, actually.

The recent two projects, my bringing Aahz back from Perv and the rest of the team trying to stop Possiltum's army, were notable exceptions. These were almost personal missions, undertaken on my own motivations or suggestions, without an actual client or revenue.

Now, however, I was confronted by an entirely new situation.

Everyone in the crew was hanging around the castle . . . with the exception of Tananda, who was minding the offices back on Deva. The question was, did they have to be here?

I had a hunch that they were mostly staying here because they were worried about me . . . not without some justification. They all knew I was in a spot, and wanted to be close at hand if I needed help.

While I appreciated their concern, and definitely wanted the moral support, I also had to admit that there wasn't whole bunches they could do. Bunny was invaluable in turning the kingdom's finances around, but aside from holding my hand through this crisis, there was relatively little the others could do.

The trouble was, by simple arithmetic, while they were here on Possiltum, they weren't out working other assignments, making money for M.Y.T.H. Inc. and therefore for themselves . . . for a whole month! On top of the work time they missed while stopping Hemlock's army as a favor to me. If this organization was going to be a functioning, profit-making venture and not a humanitarian "bail-Skeeve-out" charity, we had to get back our bottom-line orientation. What's more, both as president and the one who had led us off on this side trip, I had to seize the initiative in setting things right again. That meant that I either had to trim the force, or go along with Bunny's plan of charging the kingdom for all our time.

The question was, who to trim?

Aahz had to stay. Not only had I just gone through a lot of trouble to get him back from Perv, but I genuinely valued his advice and guidance. While I had gotten into immeasurably more trouble since we first met, I had also become very aware that he was unequaled at getting us *out* of trouble as well.

Bunny was a must. Even though it had been Tananda's idea originally to deal her in on this mess, I was very aware that without her expertise and knowledge, we didn't have a chance at bailing out the kingdom financially. Besides, judging by her greeting when we were reunited, I wasn't sure she'd be willing to go back to the Bazaar and leave me to face this dilemma alone.

As to my three bodyguards . . . after a moment's thought I decided to hold judgment on that one. First of all, I had just convinced Pookie to stay, which would make me look like a fool if I suddenly changed my mind. Second, I wasn't altogether sure I wouldn't need them. When I went off to Perv, I did it without Guido and Nunzio . . . over their strong protests . . . and ended up having to hire Pookie in their absence. Before I thought seriously about sending them all away again, I'd want to have a long talk about how *they* viewed my prospective danger here. While I wanted to save the kingdom money, I wasn't so generous as to do it if it meant putting myself in danger.

That left Massha and Chumley.

Massha came to me as an apprentice, and though I hadn't been very diligent in teaching her magik, I still had a responsibility to her that couldn't be filled if she were on Deva and I was here. Despite the fact I hadn't let her accompany me to Perv, I knew full well from my own experience that an apprentice's place is with his or her teacher.

I was suddenly confronted by the fact that the only one remaining on the list to be trimmed was Chumley . . . and I didn't want to do it. Despite the hairyknuckled, muscle-bound illiterate act the troll like to put on when he was working, Chumley was probably the levelest head in our entire M.Y.T.H. Inc. crew. Frankly, I trusted his judgment and wisdom a lot more than I did Aahz's fiery temper. The idea of trying to make up my mind about Queen Hemlock's proposal without Chumley's wisdom was disquieting at best. Maybe *after* I had reached my decision . . .

As much as I had tried to avoid thinking about it, the problem popped into my head and the potential ramifications hit me with a chilling impact.

Nervously, I gulped down the remaining wine in my goblet and hastily refilled it.

After I reached my decision . . .

44

All my thoughts and energies were focused on the immediate problems and short term plans. What was going to happen *after* I made my decision, whatever that decision was?

Things were never going to be the same for me.

Whether I married Queen Hemlock or, if refused, she abdicated and left me to run the kingdom on my own, I was going to be committed to stay in Possiltum a long time. A *very* long time.

I couldn't do that and maintain an office on Deva!

Would we have to move our operation here to Klah?

For that matter, could I be either a consort or a king and still do a responsible job as the president of M.Y.T.H. Inc.?

If I was uneasy about charging the kingdom for my crew for a month, how could I justify putting them all on the payroll *permanently?*

What about our other commitments? If we moved to Klah, it would mean giving up our juicy contract with the Devan Merchant's Association as magicians in residence. Could I charge Possiltum enough to make up for that kind of an income loss?

. . . Or would I have to step down as president of M.Y.T.H. Inc. entirely? Despite my occasional complaining, I had grown to like my position, and was reluctant to give it up . . . particulary if it meant losing all my friends like Aahz and . . .

AAHZ!

However it went, would Aahz want to hang around as a partner constantly standing in the shadow of my being consort or king? Having just recently dealt with his pride head to head, I doubted it very much.

Whatever my decision, the odds were that, once I reached it, I was going to lose Aahz!

A soft rap on my door interrupted my thoughts.

"Say, Boss. Can you spare a minute?"

Not only could I spare it, I was glad for the break.

"Sure Guido. Come on in. Pour yourself some wine."

"I never drink when I'm workin,' Boss," he said with a hint of reproach, "but thanks anyway. I just need to talk to you about something."

My senior bodyguard took a chair and sat fidgeting with the roll of parchment he was holding. It occurred to me how seldom I just sat and talked with my bodyguards. I had rather gotten accustomed to their just being there.

"So, what can I do for you?" I said, sipping my wine casually, trying to put him at his ease.

"Well, Boss," he began hesitantly, "it's like this. I was thinkin' . . . You know how Nunzio and me spent some time in the army here?"

"Yes, I heard about that."

"Bein' on the inside like that, I get the feelin' I probably know a little more'n you do about the army types and how they think. The truth is, I'm a little worried about how they're gonna handle bein' tax collectors. Know what I mean?"

"Not really," I admitted.

"What I mean is," Guido continued earnestly, "when you're a soldier, you don't have to worry much about how popular you are with the enemy, 'cause mostly you're tryin' to make him dead and you don't expect him to like it. It's different doin' collection work, whether it's protection money or taxes, which is of course just a different kind of protection racket. Ya gotta be more diplomatic 'cause you're gonna have to deal with the same people over and over again. These army types might be aces when it comes to takin' real estate away from a rival operation, but I'm not sure how good they are at knowin' when to be gentle with civilian types. Get my drift?"

While I had never shared Guido's experience of being *in* an army, I had faced one once during my first assignment here at the court of Possiltum, and even earlier had been lynched by some soldiers acting as city guardsmen. Now, suddenly, I had visions of army troops with crossbows and catapults advancing on helpless citizens.

"I hadn't really thought about it," I said, "but I see your point."

"Well, you know I don't care much for meddlin' in management type decisions," Guido continued, "but I have a sugges-

46

tion. I was thinkin' you could maybe appoint someone from the army to specifically inspect and investigate the collectin' process. You know, to be sure the army types didn't get too carried away with their new duties."

I really appreciated Guido's efforts to come up with a solution, particularly as I didn't have one of my own. Unfortunately, there seemed to be a bit of a flaw in his logic.

"Um . . . I don't quite understand, Guido," I said. "Isn't it kind of pointless to have someone from the army watching over the army? I mean, what's to say our inspector will be any different from the one's he's supposed to be policing?"

"Two things," my bodyguard replied, flashing his smile for the first time since he entered the room. "First, I have someone specific in mind for the inspector . . . one of my old army buddies. Believe me, Boss, this person is not particularly fond or tolerant of the way the army does things. As a matter of fact, I've already had the papers drawn up to formalize the assignment. All you gotta do is sign 'em."

He passed me the scroll he had been clutching and I realized he had actually been thinking out this suggestion well in advance.

"Funny name for a soldier," I said, scanning the document. "Spyder."

"Trust me, Boss," Guido pressed. "This is the person for the job."

"You said there were two things?" I stalled. "What's the other?"

"Well, I thought you could have a couple personal envoys tag along. You know, reportin' directly to you. That way you could be doubly sure the army wasn't hidin' anything from you."

"I see," I said, toying with the scroll. "And I suppose you have a couple specific people in mind for the envoys, as well?"

"Um . . . As a matter of fact . . ."

"I don't know, Guido," I said, shaking my head. "I mean, it's a good idea, but I'm not sure I can spare both you and Nunzio. If nothing else, I want Nunzio to do a little work with Gleep. I want to find out for sure if there's anything wrong with him."

"Ah . . . Actually, Boss," my bodyguard said, carefully studying his massive hands, "I wasn't thinkin' of Nunzio. I was thinkin' maybe Pookie and me could handle it."

More than anything else he had said, this surprised me. Guido and his cousin Nunzio had always worked as a team, to a point where I practically thought of the two of them as one person. The fact that Guido was willing to split the team up was an indication of how concerned he was over the situation. Either that, or a sign of how far he was willing to go to get some time alone with Pookie.

"Really, Boss," he urged, sensing my hesitation. "There ain't a whole lot to do here for three bodyguards. I mean, the way I see it, the only one here in the castle who might want to do you any bodily harm is the Queen herself, and I don't think you have to worry about her until after you've made up your mind on the marriage thing. I'm just lookin' for a way that we can earn our keep . . . something useful to do."

That did it. His point about reassigning my bodyguards played smack into my current thinking about trimming the team or expanding their duties. Then, too, I wasn't eager to prolong any discussion which involved my making up my mind about what to do about Hemlock.

"Okay, Guido," I said, scribbling my signature across the bottom of the scroll. "You've got it. Just be sure to keep me posted as to what's going on."

"Thanks, Boss," he grinned, taking the scroll and looking at the signature. "You won't regret this."

It hadn't occurred to me at all that I might regret it . . . until he mentioned it. I mean, what could go wrong?

Chapter Six

"Money is the root of all evil. Women need roots."
D. Trump

T hough the various administrative hassles of trying to straighten out Possiltum's finances weighed heavily on my mind, there was another, bigger worry that ran like an undercurrent through my head whenever I was awake.

Should I or shouldn't I marry Queen Hemlock?

Aahz kept saying that I should go along with it, become the royal consort with an easy (not to mention well paying) job for life. I had to admit, in many ways it looked more attractive than having her abdicate and ending up holding the bag for running the kingdom all by myself. I had that "opportunity" once before courtesy of the late King Roderick, and *really* didn't want to repeat the experience.

So why was I dragging my feet on making my decision?

Mostly, my indecision was due to my reluctance to accept the obvious choice. As much as I was repelled by the known quantity of being king, I was as much or more terrified of the unknown factors involved in marriage.

Time and time again, I tried to sort out if it was the idea of getting married that scared me, or if it was Queen Hemlock specifically that I couldn't picture as my wife.

My *wife!*

Every time that phrase crossed my mind, it was like an icy hand grabbed my heart hard enough to make it skip a beat.

Frankly, I was having trouble picturing *anyone* I knew in that role. In an effort to get a handle on my feelings, I forced myself to review the women of my acquaintance in that light.

Massha, my apprentice, was out of the question. While we were close enough as friends, as well as teacher/student, her sheer size was intimidating. The truth was, I had trouble thinking of her as a woman. Oh, I knew she was female all right, but I tended to see her as a friend who was female . . . not as a *female,* if you can see the difference.

Bunny . . . well, I supposed that she could be considered a candidate. The problem there was that she was the first woman who had made a solid pass at me, and it had scared me to death. When her uncle, Don Bruce, first dumped her on me, she was all set to play a gangster's moll. Once I got her straightened out, however, she had settled into being my administrative assistant like a duck takes to water, and the question of anything intimate developing between us never came up again. Thinking of her in terms of a life partner would mean completely restructuring how I viewed her and worked with her, and right now she was far too valuable as my assistant for me to rock the boat.

Tananda . . . I had to smile at the thought of the Trollop assassin as my wife. Oh, she was friendly enough, not to mention very attractive, and for a long time I had a crush on her. It eventually became apparent, however, that the hugs and kisses she bestowed on me were no different than those she gave the rest of the team . . . including her brother Chumley. She was just a physically friendly person, and the affection she showed me was that shown for a co-worker, or maybe a kid brother. I could accept that, now. Besides, I somehow couldn't see her giving up her own career to settle down keeping house for me. No, as much as I loved her,

Tananda would never fit as my wife. She was . . . well, Tananda.

That left Queen Hemlock, who I had no real feeling for at all except, perhaps a sense of uneasiness every time she was around. She always seemed extremely sure of herself and what she wanted . . . which made her almost my exact opposite. Of course, that in itself was an interesting thought. Then, too, she was the only one who had ever expressed a desire to be paired with me . . . and seemed to want it badly enough to fight for it. Even Bunny had backed off once I rebuffed her. I had to admit that it did something to a man's ego to have a woman determined to bag him . . . even if he wasn't all that drawn to the woman in the first place.

Unfortunately, that was pretty much it for my list of female acquaintances. Oh, there were a few others I had come into contact with over the years, like Markie . . . and Luanna . . .

Luanna!!

She had almost slipped my mind completely, but once I thought of her, her face sprang into focus as if she were standing in front of me. Luanna. Lovely Luanna. Our paths had only crossed a couple times, most notably during my adventure in the dimension of Limbo, and the last time we met the parting hadn't been pleasant. In short, I really didn't know her at all. Still, in many ways, she epitomized everything that was feminine in my mind. Not only did she radiate a soft, vulnerable beauty, her manner was demure. That may not seem like much to you, but it was to me. You see, most of the women I work with can only be called aggressive . . . or, less politely, brassy. Even Hemlock, for all her regal blood, was very straightforward about stating her mind and wishes. Bunny had cooled it a bit, once I got her off her moll kick, but had replaced her blatant suggestiveness with a brusk efficient manner that, at times, could be every bit as intimidating as her old sex kitten routine.

In contrast, Luanna always seemed very shy and hesitant in my presence. Her voice was usually quiet to a point I sometimes had to strain to hear her, and she had a habit of looking down, then peering up at me through her lashes . . . as if she felt I could bully her physically or verbally, but trusted me not to. I can't speak for other men, but it always made me feel ten feet tall . . . very powerful and with an overwhelming urge to use that strength to protect her from the hardships of the world.

Thinking of her while trying to appraise what I would want in a wife, I found myself dwelling on the image of finding her waiting for me at the close of each day . . . and realized the image wasn't all that objectionable. In fact, once she surfaced in my memory, I found myself thinking of her quite a bit whenever I tried to sort out my current position, and more than occasionally wished I could see her again before I had to make my final decision.

As it turned out, I got my wish.

I was in my room, making another of my feeble attempts to make head or tail of the stack of spread sheets that Bunny and Grimble kept passing me on an almost daily basis. As those of you who have been following these adventures from the beginning may recall, I *can* read . . . or, at least, I had *thought* that I could. Since undertaking the task of sorting out the kingdom's finances, however, I had found out that reading text, which is to say, words, is a *lot* different that being able to read numbers.

I mean, we were all in agreement as to our goal, which was to eliminate or lessen the kingdom's debt load without either placing a staggering tax burden on the populace *or* cutting so much off the operating budget that the necessary administrative operations became non-functional. As I say, we were all in agreement . . . verbally . . . with words. Any time there was a disagreement between Grimble and Bunny on particulars, however, and they came to me to cast the deciding vote or make a decision, they would each invariably support their side of the argument by passing me one or more of those cryptic sheets covered with numbers and not much else, then wait expectantly as I scanned it, as if their case had just become self-explanatory.

Now, for those of you who have never been placed in this situation, let me offer a little clarification. When I say I can't read numbers, I don't mean that I can't decipher the symbols. I *know* what a two is and what it stands for and how it differs from, say, an eight. The problem I was confronted with in these arguments was trying to see them in relation to each other. To do a "word analogy," if the numbers were words, both Bunny and Grimble could look at a page full of numbers and see sentences and paragraphs, complete with subtleties and innuendos, whereas I would look at the same page and see a mass of unrelated, individual words. This was particularly uncomfortable when they would pass me two pages of what to them was a mystery novel, and ask my opinion on who the killer was.

Even though I *knew* they knew I was a numeric illiterate, I had gotten awfully tired of saying "Duh, I don't know" in varying forms, and, in an effort to salvage a few shreds of my self-respect, had taken to saying instead "Let me look these over and get back to you." Unfortunately, this meant that at any specific point in time, I had a batch of these "mystery sheets" on my desk that I felt obligated to at least *try* to make sense of.

Anyhoo, that's what I was doing when a knock came at my door. In short, I was feeling inept, frustrated, and desperately in need of diversion.

"Yes?" I called eagerly, hoping beyond hope that it was news of an earthquake or attacking army or something equally disastrous that would require my immediate attention. "Who is it?"

The door opened, and Massha's head appeared.

"You busy, Hot Stuff?" she said with the respect and deference she always shows me as my apprentice. "You've got a visitor."

"Nothing that can't wait, I replied, hastily stacking the offensive spreadsheets and replacing them in their customary spot on the corner of my desk. "Who's the visitor?"

"It's Luanna. You remember, the babe who almost got us killed over in Limbo?"

In hindsight, I can see that Massha was both expressing her disapproval and trying to warn me with her description of Luanna, but at the time it didn't register at all.

"Luanna?" I said, beaming with delight. "Sure, bring her in. Better yet, *send* her in."

"Don't worry," Massha sniffed, disdainfully. "I wouldn't *dream* of intruding on your little tete-a-tete."

Again, her reaction escaped my notice. I was far to busy casting about the room quickly to be sure it was presentable . . . which, of course, it was. If nothing else, the maid service in the castle was stellar.

And she was there . . . standing in my room, as lovely and winsome as I remembered.

"Uh . . . Hi, Luanna," I said, suddenly at a loss for words.

"Skeeve," she said in that soft, low voice that seemed to make the simplest statements an exercise in eloquence.

We looked at each other in silence for a few moments.

Then, suddenly, it occurred to me that the last time we saw each other, she had left in a huff under the misapprehension that I was married and had a kid.

"About the last . . ." I began.

"I'm sorry about . . ." she stated simultaneously.

We both broke off abruptly, then looked at each other and laughed.

"Okay. You first." I said finally, with a half bow.

"I just wanted to apologize for the way I acted the last time we were together. What I heard later from the rumor mill at the Bazaar convinced me that things weren't what they seemed at the time, and I felt terrible about not having given you a chance to explain. I should have looked you up sooner to say how sorry I was, but I wasn't sure you'd even want to talk to me again. I . . . I only hope you can forgive me . . . even though there's no real reason you should . . ."

Her voice trailed off as she dropped her eyes.

Looking the way she did, so demure, so defenseless, I could have forgiven her for being a mass murderess, much less for any minor misunderstanding between us.

"Don't worry about it," I said, in what I hoped was an offhand manner. "Truth to tell, Luanna, I was about to apologize to you.

It must have been terrible for you . . . coming to me for help and walking into the . . . ah . . . situation you did. I've been thinking that I should have handled it a lot better than I did."

That's so sweet of you, Skeeve," Luanna said, stepping forward to give me a quick hug and a peck of a kiss. "You don't know how glad I am to hear you say that."

Not surprisingly, her brief touch did strange things to my mind . . . and metabolism. It was only the second time she had kissed me and the other time I had been into the middle of conning her out of a handkerchief so I could get Aahz out of jail. All of which is to say I was far from immune to her kisses, however casual.

"So . . . ah . . .What brings you to Possiltum?" I said, fighting to keep my reactions from showing.

"Why, you of course."

"Me?"

Despite my feigned surprise, I felt my pulse quicken. I mean, I could have assumed that she was here to see me, but it was nice to have it confirmed that I was the sole purpose of her visit rather than a polite afterthought.

"Sure. I heard about your new position here, and figured it was too good a chance to pass up."

That didn't sound quite so good.

"Excuse me?"

"Oh, I'm getting it all turned around," she said, cutely annoyed with herself. "What I'm trying to say is that I have a proposal for you."

That was better. In fact, it was a little too good to be true. While I had been indulging my fantasies about Luana as a possible wife, I never dared to think that she might be thinking the same thoughts about me . . . as a husband, I mean, not a wife.

"A proposal?" I said, deliberately stalling to organize my thoughts.

"That's right. I figure that you've probably got a bit of discretionary funds available now that you're on the kingdom payroll, and the kind of scams I run have a good return on investment, so I was hoping that I could get a little start-up money from you and . . ."

Whoa! Stop the music!"

It had taken a few beats for what she was saying to sink in, obsessed as I was with my own expectations of the conversation. Even now, with my pretty dream-bubble exploding around me, I was having trouble changing gears mentally to focus on what she was actually getting at.

"Could you back up and take it from the top? You're here to ask for money?"

"Well. . . . Yes. Not much really . . . maybe fifty or seventy-five in gold should do." she clarified hastily. "The nice thing with scams is they don't really need much up-front capital."

"You mean you want to borrow money from me so you can run a swindle? Here, in Possiltum?"

The look she leveled on me was, to say the least, cold and appraising. Not at all the coy, shy, averted gaze I was used to from her.

"Of course. That's what I do," she said levelly. "I thought you knew that when you offered me a job. Or are you just miffed because I prefer to operate independently? I suppose this is pretty small potatoes to you, but it's the best I can do."

As she spoke, my mind was racing back over the previous times I had seen or spoken with her. While I was aware then that she was always involved in or running from the results of some swindle or other, I had always assumed that she was a sweet kid who was going along with her partner, Matt. I realized now that I had no basis on which to make that assumption, other than her innocent looks. If fact, beyond her looks, I really didn't know her at all.

"Is it?" I said. "Is it really the best you can do?"

What do you mean?"

"Well, couldn't you do as well or better trying your hand at something legitimate? What if I passed you enough money to start and run a normal business?"

56

The last vestige of my idealized fantasies regarding Luanna died as her lip curled in a sneer.

"You mean run a little shop or grocery store? Me? No thanks. That's *way* too much like work. Funny, I always thought that if *anyone* would understand that, *you* would. You didn't get where you are today by hard work and sweat, you did it by fleecing the gullible and flim-flamming the ignorant, just like Matt and I did . . . just on a larger scale. Of course, we didn't have a demon helping us along, like you did. Even now, as rich and respectable as you're supposed to be, I'll bet you're pulling down a healthy skim from this kingdom. It's got to be real easy, what with having the Queen in your pocket and everybody doing whatever you say. All I'm trying to do is to cut myself in for a piece of the action . . . and a little piece, at that."

I was silent for a few moments. I thought of trying to tell her about the long hours and work I and my team were putting in trying to straighten out the kingdom's finances. I even considered showing her some of the cryptic spread sheets on my desk . . . but decided against it. She might be able to decipher them, and if she could would doubtless ask some embarrassing questions about the hefty fee I was taking for my services. I was having trouble justifying that to myself, much less to her.

The inescapable conclusion, however, was that no matter what I had thought lovely Luanna was like, we were worlds apart in our views of people and how they should be treated.

Reaching into our petty cash drawer, I started counting out some coins.

"Tell you what, Luanna," I said, not looking up. "You said you needed fifty to seventy-five in gold? Well I'm going to give you a hundred and fifty . . . double to triple what you asked for . . . not as a loan or an investment, just as a gift."

"But why would you . . . "

". . . There *are* two conditions, though," I continued, as if she hadn't spoken. "First, that you use some of the extra money for travel. Go off dimension or to another part of Klah . . . I don't care. Just so long as when you start to run your swindle, it's not in Possiltum."

"Okay, but . . . "

"And second," I said, setting the stack of coins on the edge of the desk near her, "I want you to promise that you will never see or speak to me . . . ever again . . . starting now."

For a moment, I thought she was going to speak. She opened her mouth, then hesitated, shrugged, and shut it again. In complete silence she gathered up the coins and left, shutting the door behind her.

I poured myself another goblet of wine and moved to the window, staring out at the view without really seeing anything. Dreams die hard, but whatever romantic thoughts I had ever had involving Luanna had just been squashed pretty thoroughly. I couldn't change that, but I could mourn their passing.

There was a soft knock at the door, and my heart took a sudden leap. Maybe she had changed her mind! Maybe she had thought it over and decided to return the money in favor of a legitimate business loan!

"Come in," I called, trying not to sound to eager.

The door opened, and a vampire walked in.

Chapter Seven

"You Just don't know women."
H. Hefner

"**W**ine? No thanks. Never touch the stuff."

"Oh. That's right. Sorry, Vic," I said, refilling my own goblet.

"You know," my guest said, settling himself more comfortably in his seat, "It's women like Luanna that give vampires a bad name. *They're* the ones who will mercilessly suck someone dry, and the concept sort of slopped over onto us!"

In case you're wondering (or have neglected to read the earlier books in this series), Vic is the one who walked into my room at the end of the last chapter, and yes he *is* a vampire. Actually, he's a pretty nice guy . . . about my age and a fairly successful magician in his own right. He just happens to come from Limbo, a dimension that's primarily "peopled" by vampires, werewolves, and the like.

Apparently he had stopped by our office on Deva looking to invite me out for lunch. When Tananda, who was currently minding the fort for us, told him where I was, he decided to pop over for a visit. (As an aside, one of his Limbo-born talents is the ability to travel the dimension without mechanical aid . . . something I've always envied and wanted to learn.)

Truth to tell, I was more than a little glad to see Vic. He was one of the few in my acquaintance who was familiar with the trials and tribulations of being a professional magician, yet wasn't an actual member of our crew. Not meaning any disrespect or criticism of my colleagues, mind you, but . . . well . . . they were more like family and my actions and future definitely affected them, whereas Vic was a bit more able to stand apart and view things objectively. This made it a lot easier to express my feelings and problems to him, which I had proceeded to do, starting with Queen Hemlock's proposal and running it right up through my recent rather disheartening meeting with Luanna.

Until he brought it up, I had forgotten that he had met Luanna. In fact, he had worked with her and Matt, and consequently gone on the lam with them . . . which was when I met him in the first place. As such, he knew the lady under discussion far better than I did, and my new analysis of her seemed more in line with his earlier formed opinions than with my own cherished daydreams.

"I can't say much about what you're doing with the kingdom's budgets and stuff," the vampire said with an easy shrug. "That's out of my league. It *does* occur to me, though, that you're having more than your share of woman problems."

"You can say that again," I agreed, toasting him with my goblet.

"I'll admit I'm a bit surprised," Vic continued. "I would have thought that someone with your experience would have been able to side-step some of these tangles . . . and definitely spotted a gold-digger like Luanna a mile away."

I hesitated for a moment, then decided to level with him.

"To be honest with you, Vic, I haven't had all that much experience with women."

"Really?" The vampire was gratifyingly surprised.

"Let's just say that while Aahz and the others have been fairly diligent about teaching me the ins and outs of business and magik, there have been certain areas of my education that have been woefully and annoyingly neglected."

"Now *that* I might be able to help you with."

"Excuse me?"

I had been momentarily lost in my own thoughts, and had somehow missed a turn in the conversation.

"It's easy," Vic said with a shrug. "You're having trouble making up your mind whether or not you should get married at all . . . much less to Queen Hemlock. Right?"

"Well . . . "

"Right?" he pressed.

"Right."

"To me, the problem is that you don't have enough information to make an educated decision."

"You can say that again," I said heavily, gulping at my wine. "What's more, between the workload here and Queen Hemlock's timetable, I don't figure I'm going to get any, either."

"*That's* where I think I can help you," my guest smiled, leaning back in his chair again.

"Excuse me?" I said, fighting off the feeling that our conversation was caught in an unending loop.

"What would you say to a blind date?"

That one caught me totally off guard.

"Well . . . the same thing I'd say to a date that could see, I imagine," I managed at last. "The trouble is, I haven't had any experience with either . . . "

"No, no," the vampire interrupted. "I mean, how would you like me to fix you up with a date? Someone you've never seen before?"

"That would have to be the case," I nodded. "I don't recall ever having *met* a blind person . . . male or female. Not that I've consciously avoided them, mind you . . . "

"Hold it! Stop!" Vic said, holding up one hand while pressing the other to his forehead.

It occurred to me that, in that pose, he looked more than a little like Aahz.

"Let's try this again . . . from the top. We were talking about your needing more experience with women. What I'm suggesting is that I line you up with a date . . . someone I know . . . so you can get that experience. Got it?"

"Got it," I nodded. "*You* know someone who's blind. Tell me, should I act any different around her?"

"No . . . . I mean, yes! NO!"

Vic seemed to be getting very worked up over the subject, and more than a little confused . . . which made two of us.

"Look, Skeeve," he said finally through clenched teeth. "The girl I'm thinking about is *not* blind. She's perfectly normal. Okay?"

"Okay," I said, hesitantly, looking for the hook. "A perfectly normal, average girl."

"Well . . . not all *that* normal, or average," the vampire smiled, relaxing a bit. "She's a *lot* of fun . . . if you get what I mean. And she's a real looker . . . knock your eyes out beautiful."

"You mean *I'll* go blind?"

Out of my merciful nature and in the interest of brevity (too late), I'll spare you the blow by blow account of the rest of the conversation. Let it suffice to say that, by the time Vic departed, it had been established that he would arrange for me to step out with a lovely lady of his acquaintance . . . one who was in full command of her senses . . . sort of (that part still confused me a little) . . . and who would not adversely affect my health or senses, but would, if Vic were to be believed, advance my education regarding the opposite sex to dizzying heights.

It sounded good to me. Like any healthy young man, I had a normal interest in women . . . which is to say I didn't think of them more than three or four times a day. My lack of first hand experience I attributed to a dearth of opportunity, which apparently was about to be remedied. To say I was looking forward to my date would be an understatement . . . a VAST understatement.

However the events of the day weren't over yet.

There was a knock at the door, but this time I wasn't

going to get caught making any assumptions.

"Who is it?" I called.

"General Badaxe," came the muffled response. "I was wondering if you could spare me a moment?"

I was more than a little surprised. The General and I had never been on particularly good terms, and it was rare if ever that he called on me in my personal quarters. Casting about for an explanation, it occurred to me that he was probably more than a little upset at the cutbacks I had made in the army and military budget. In the same thought, it occurred to me that he might be out to murder me in my own room . . . or, at least, mess me up a little. As fast as the idea surfaced, however, I discarded it. Whatever else the General was, he was as straightforward and non-scheming as anyone I had ever met. If he meant to do me harm, it would doubtless be on the spur of the moment when we encountered each other in the halls or courtyard of the castle . . . not by stealth in my room. In short, I felt I could rule out premeditated mayhem. If he were going to kill me, it would be spontaneous . . . a thought that didn't settle my mind as much as I hoped it would.

"Come in," I called . . . and he did.

It was, indeed, the General of Possiltum's army, and without his namesake massive axe, for a change. Not that it's absence made him noticeably less dangerous, mind you, as Badaxe was easily the largest man I had ever met. Upon viewing him, however, I was a bit embarrassed by my original worries. Rather than the stern, angry countenance I was accustomed to, he seemed very ill at ease and uncomfortable.

"Sorry to interrupt your work, Lord Magician," he said, nervously looking about the room, "but I find it necessary to speak to you on . . . a personal matter."

"Certainly, General," I said, trying to put him at his ease. Strangely, I found that his obvious discomfort was making me uneasy. "Have a seat."

"Thank you, I'd rather stand."

So much for putting him at ease.

"As you wish," I nodded. "What is it you wanted to see me about?"

I realized with some chagrin that I was falling into a formal speech pattern, but found that I couldn't help it. Badaxe seemed bound and determined to be somber, and I felt obligated to respond in kind.

"Well . . . I'd like to speak to you about your apprentice."

"Aahz?" I said. As far as the kingdom was concerned, Aahz was my loyal student.

"What's he done now?"

"No . . . not Aahz." the General clarified hastily. "I was referring to Massha."

"Massha?" I blinked. This was truly a surprise. As far as I knew, Massha and the General had always gotten along fine. "Very well. What's the problem?

"Oh, don't understand me, Lord Magician. There's no problem. Quite the contrary. I wanted to speak to you taking her hand in marriage."

On a day of surprises, this announcement caught me the most off guard.

"Why?" I sputtered, unable to think of anything else to say.

The General's brow darkened noticeably.

"If you're referring to her less than slender appearance, or perhaps the difference in our age . . . " he began in a deep growl.

"No, you misunderstand me," I said hastily, cutting him off . . . though once he mentioned them, both points were worth reflecting on. "I meant, why should you want to speak to *me* about such a matter?"

"Oh. That."

For the moment, at least, Badaxe seemed mollified. I mentally made a note to table any discussion of the two points he had raised until another time.

"It's really rather simple, Lord Magician," the General was continuing. "Though I suppose it's rather old fashioned of me, I felt I should follow proprieties and establish my good intentions by stating them in advance. Normally I'd speak to her father, but, in this case, you seem to be the closest thing to a father she has."

Now I was truly flabbergasted. Mostly because, try as I might, I couldn't find a hole in his logic. He was right. Even though she was older than me, Massha had never spoken of her family at all . . . much less a father. What was more, this was one I couldn't even fob off on Aahz. Since she was *my* apprentice, I was responsible for her care and well-being as well as her training. If there was anyone the General should speak to on matters regarding Massha's future, it was me!

"I see," I said, stalling for time to think. "And what does Massha have to say about this?"

"So far, I haven't spoken to her directly on the subject," Badaxe admitted uneasily, "though I have reason to believe the idea wouldn't be totally unwelcome to her. Frankly, I felt that I should attempt to gain your approval first."

"And why is that?"

I was getting better at this stalling game, and questions were a handy weapon.

The General eyed me levelly.

"Come, come, Lord Magician," he said. "I thought that we had long since agreed there was no need to bandy words between us. You know as well as I that Massha has a great deal of affection for you. What's more, there is the added loyalty of an apprentice to her teacher. While I have never shied from either battle or competition, I would prefer to spare her any unnecessary anguish. That is, I feel it would aid my case immensely if, at the same time I asked her to be my wife, I could state that I had spoken with you and that you had no personal or professional objections to such a match. That is, of course, assuming you don't."

I was silent for a few moments, reflecting on what he had said. Specifically, I was berating myself for being so selfish in my thinking, of only considering the consequences to *me* in my decision of whether or not to marry Queen Hemlock. Even when I had been thinking of my friends and colleagues, I had been looking at it in terms of *my* loss of their friendship, not what it might mean to them.

"Then again, perhaps I was wrong in my assumption,"

The General's words interrupted my thoughts, and I was suddenly aware that he had been waiting for a response from me.

"Forgive me, General . . . Hugh," I said hastily. I had to think quickly to recall his first name. "I was simply lost in thought for a moment. Certainly I have no objections. I've always held you in the highest regard, and, if Massha is amenable, I would be the last to stand between her and happiness. Feel free to proceed with my approval . . . and best wishes."

Badaxe seized my hand and pumped it hard . . . fortunately before I could pull it away in alarm.

"Thank you, Lord . . . Skeeve," he said with an intensity I had only seen him express in battle planning. "I . . . Thank you."

Releasing my hand, he strode to the door, opened it, then paused.

"Were it not for the fact that, assuming she agrees, of course, I expect Massha will ask you to give the bride away, I'd ask you to honor me by standing as my best man."

Then he was gone . . . which was just as well, as I had no idea what to say in response.

Massha and Badaxe. Married.

Try as I might, I couldn't get my mind around the concept . . . which is a comment on the limits of my imagination and NOT on their respective physical sizes, individually or as a twosome.

Finally, I abandoned the effort completely. Instead, I poured myself another goblet of wine and settled back for the far more pleasant exercise of speculating on my own upcoming date.

Chapter Eight

"Love is blind. Lust isn't!"
D. Giovani

I found myself experiencing mixed feelings as I prepared for my date that evening. On the one hand, I wasn't real sure about how much fun it would be spending an entire evening with a woman I had never met before. While I had a certain amount of faith in Vic not to stick me with a real loser, it occurred to me that it would be nice to have some vague idea of what she was going to look like. Heck, if she turned out to be a lousy conversationalist, the evening could still turn out okay if she was at least fun to look at.

Despite my nagging concerns, however, there was no denying I felt a certain measure of excitement as the time drew near. As Vic had observed, I didn't really have a lot of experience with dating. Specifically, this was going to be my first date . . . ever. Now don't get me wrong, I knew a fair number of women, but I had met all of them in the course of business. Before I met Aahz, I had been living alone with Garkin in a shack in the woods . . . which is not the greatest way to meet females. Since tying on with Aahz, my life had gotten noticeably more excit-

67

ing, but there was little time for a social life. What off time I did have was usually spent with other members of our crew, and while they were good company for the most part, it left little room for outsiders. Consequently, the idea of spending an entire evening with a strange woman *just to be spending time together* was a real treat . . . and more than a little scary.

The one variable in the whole situation I **could** control was me, and I was bound and determined that if anything went wrong with the evening, it wouldn't be because I hadn't put enough effort into my preparations. Money was easy. While I wasn't sure where we would be going, I figured that two or three hundred in gold would cover our expenses . . . though I made a note to bring along my credit card from Perv just to be on the safe side.

Wardrobe was another matter. After changing my outfit completely a dozen times, I finally settled on the same clothes I had worn when I had my match with the Sen-Sen Ante Kid . . . the dark maroon open necked shirt with the charcoal grey slacks and vest. I figured that if it had impressed people on Deva, it should be impressive no matter where we went. Of course, on Deva, I had also been traveling with an entourage of bodyguards and assistants . . . not to mention a quarter of a million in gold.

I was just considering changing my clothes one more time, when there was a knock at the door. This surprised me a little, as I had somehow expected that my date would simply appear in the room. As soon as that thought occurred to me, however, it also occurred to me that there had been an excellent chance that she would have appeared while I was changing outfits. Slightly relieved at having escaped a potentially embarrassing situation, I opened the door.

"Hi, Skeeve," Bunny said, sweeping past me into the room. "I thought I'd stop by and brief you on the latest budget developments and maybe do dinner and . . . Hey! You look nice."

Needless to say, this was an unexpected . . . and unpleasant . . . surprise.

"Um . . . Actually I was just getting ready to go out." I managed politely.

She took it well. In fact, she seemed to brighten at the news.

"That's a great idea!" she said. "Hang on a few and I'll duck back to my room and change and we can go out together!"

"Um . . . Bunny . . . "

"To tell you the truth, I've been starting to go up the walls a little myself. It'll be wonderful to get out for a while, especially with you, and . . . "

"BUNNY!"

She stopped and cocked her head at me.

"What is it, Skeeve?"

"I . . . actually . . . well . . . I have a date."

The words hung in the air as she stared at me with eyes that had suddenly gotten very large.

"Oh," she said finally in a small voice. "I . . . Then I guess I'd better be moving along."

"Wait a minute, Bunny," I said, catching her as she started for the door. "Maybe tomorrow we can . . . "

There was a soft "BAMPF" in the room behind us, and we turned to discover that my date had arrived . . . at least, I assumed she was my date. I could think of no other reason for a creature appearing in my room that looked like that.

She was pale, even paler than Queen Hemlock, which only served to accent the deep red lipstick she wore. She was short, though her hair nearly made up for it as it rose from the top of her head in a thick dark wave before cascading all the way down her back well past her rump. Her body was heart-stopping, abundant to the point of exaggeration on top, narrowing to an unbelievably tiny waist before flaring into her tidy hips. It would have been noticeable in any situation, but her dress made sure it wouldn't be overlooked.

It was a sparkley black, and hugged her curves like it was tattooed on. The neckline plunged daringly nearly to her navel, actually lower than the slit up the side of her dress, which in turn displayed one of the shapeliest legs it's ever

69

been my privilege to view first hand. To say the least it was a revealing outfit, and most of what it revealed was delectable.

About the only thing that wasn't visible or easily imaginable was her eyes, which were hidden by a pair of cats-eye sunglasses. As if in response to my thoughts, she removed them with a careless, graceful motion, setting them carefully atop her hairdo. I would have watched the action more carefully if I hadn't been staring at her eyes. It wasn't the heavy purple eye shadow that held my attention, it was the fact that the whites of her eyes were, in fact, blood red.

My date was a vampire.

I guess I should have expected it. I mean, what with Vic being a vampire, it was only predictable that he would line me up with another vampire for a date. It just hadn't been predicted by me!

"Hi!" the vision of loveliness smiled, showing a pair of sharp canine teeth. "I'm Cassandra. You must be Vic's friend."

"Good God!" Bunny said, the words escaping from her in a gasp as she stared at my visitor.

"And who's this?" Cassandra said, sweeping Bunny with a withering gaze. "The warm-up act? You must be quite a tiger to book two dates, one after the other . . . or is she coming along with us?"

"Cassandra, this is Bunny . . . my administrative assistant," I intervened hastily. "We were just going over some office matters."

This seemed to mollify Cassandra somewhat. At least enough so that she stepped forward and coiled around my arm, pressing close against me. Very close.

"Well, don't wait up for him, Sugar," she said with a wink. "I figure on keeping him up for a long time . . . if you get what I mean."

"Don't worry. I won't."

Chumley had once tried to describe something called "dry ice" to me. At the time, I had trouble imagining something cold enough to burn. Bunny's tone and manner as she spun on her heel and marched out of the room went a long way toward clarifying the concept for me. I might not be the most perceptive person in all the dimensions when it comes to women, but it didn't take a real genius to realize that she didn't approve of my choice of dates . . . even though I hadn't really made the choice.

"Alone at last," Cassandra purred, pressing even closer against me. "Tell me, Tiger, what are your thoughts for the evening?"

As I said, I hadn't really settled on anything. Still, I had an overwhelming urge to get this particular bombshell out of the castle, or, at least, out of my bedroom, and as far away from Bunny as possible.

"I don't know," I said. "I was thinking of maybe doing dinner or getting a couple of drinks and kind of letting the evening take care of itself."

"Sounds good to me," my date declared, giving a little shiver that seemed to take her entire body. "Are there any good clubs on this dimension?"

It only took me a second to realize she was talking about nightclubs, not the kind of club you beat people across the head with. I DO catch on eventually.

"I'm not sure," I admitted. "My work doesn't leave me much time to check out the night life."

"Hey! When it comes to night life, I'm your girl. I know some GREAT places over on Limbo."

Limbo! The dimension of werewolves and vampires. I had only been there once, and the memory wasn't all that pleasant.

"Um, I rather not if you don't mind."

"Really? Why not?"

"Well . . . if you must know, my dimension traveling skills aren't all they could be," I said, blurting out the first thing that came into my mind. Actually, my ability to travel the dimensions without the mechanical aid of a D-Hopper was nonexistent, but I saw no need to be *too* honest.

"If that's the only hitch, no problem," Cassandra said. "Just leave the driving to me, Tiger."

So saying, she hooked one arm in mine, did something I couldn't see with her other hand, and, before I had the chance to protest further, we were there!

Now, for those of you who have never been there (which, I assume, includes most of my readers) Limbo isn't much of a dimension to look at. That is, it's hard to see much of anything because it's DARK. Now, I don't mean "dark," I mean **DARK!!** Even when the sun is up, which it currently wasn't, it doesn't push much light through the perpetually overcast sky. Then, too, the predominant color of the architecture, roads, etc. is black, which does nothing toward brightening up the landscape. That in itself might make things look bleak, but when you added in the decorative flourishes the place looked positively **grim.**

Everywhere you looked there were gargoyles, dragons, and snakes . . . stone ones, fortunately . . . peering back at you from rooftops, balconies, and window ledges. Normally I don't mind such creatures. Heck, as you know I have a dragon of my own, and Gus is one of my best friends even though he is a gargoyle. It should be noted, however, that those individuals manage to maintain their relationship with me without constantly displaying their teeth in bloodthirsty glee, a courtesy which their stone counterparts here in Limbo did NOT extend.

Then, too, there were the bats.

For every one of the aforementioned frightful creatures, there must have been ten or twenty bat decorations on display. They came in all sizes, shapes, and poses, and seemed to have only one characteristic in common . . . none of them looked friendly. It was an unnerving reminder that a goodly proportion of the dimension's inhabitants were vampires.

"Umm . . . Is this Blut, by any chance?" I said, ostensibly studying the buildings around us while, in actuality, sneaking sideways peeks at Cassandra, trying to get another peek at her teeth.

"As a matter of fact, it is!" my date confirmed. "Don't tell me you've heard of it?"

"Actually, I've been here before."

"Really? That's strange . . . but then again, Vic *did* say that you were better traveled and informed than most off-worlders." Cassandra seemed genuinely impressed. "So, what did you think of the place?"

"I didn't really get to see much of it," I admitted. "I was sort of here on business and didn't have much time for socializing or sightseeing."

Again, this was a bit of an understatement. I had been here trying to bust Aahz out of jail before they executed him for murder. It occurred to me, however, that it might not be wise to go into too many details of my previous visit. Fortunately, I needn't have worried.

"Well we can fix that right now," Cassandra declared, grabbing my hand and pulling me along behind her as she started off. "There's a little club around the corner here that's all the rage currently. It's as good a place as any to start our expedition."

"Wait a minute," I said, digging in my heels a bit. "What about me? I mean, if I recall correctly, off-worlders in general and humans specifically aren't all that welcome here. In fact, don't most vampires consider us humans to be monsters?"

"Oh, that's just the superstitious old fuddy-duddies," my date insisted, continuing to tow me along. "The kind of folks that hang out at the clubs are pretty open minded. You'll see."

Somehow, the phrase "pretty open minded" didn't suffice to calm all my fears. I was all too aware that I was a long way from home with no independent means to get there if anything went wrong and I got separated from my date. Just to be on the safe side, I started casting about for force lines . . . the energy source I was trained to tap into for my magik. Limbo was notoriously short on them, which had caused me no small amount of problems during my last visit, and if I was going to have to do anything on "reserve power," I'd be wise to start mustering it well in advance of any trouble.

"There it is now!" Cassandra chirped, interrupting my concentration.

The place she had selected was easy to spot. It had a line of customers out front that stretched to the corner and around it. It also, however, had a strong force line running right over it, which made me much more willing to agree to it as a relaxing stop on our tour.

"Darn it!" my date said, slowing slightly. "I was afraid this would happen, what with us showing up so late and all. How are you fixed for cash, Tiger? A little palm grease could cut our wait time a bit."

"Well, all I have is a couple hundred in gold," I said hesitantly. "If that's not enough, we can always . . . "

"Whoa!" Cassandra stopped in her tracks. "Did you say a couple *hundred?*"

"That's right," I nodded, letting go of her hand to reach for my belt pouch. "I wasn't sure how much . . . "

"Don't show it around here!" my date gasped, quickly stopping my hand with her own. "Geez! Do you want to get mugged? What are you doing, carrying your whole bankroll around with you? Don't you believe in banks?"

"Sure I do," I said, a little hurt. "This is just mad money. I wasn't sure how much this evening was going to cost, so I brought a long a couple hundred . . . that and a credit card."

"Really?" she said, obviously impressed. "How much do you . . . never mind. None of my business. Vic never said you were *rich*, though. I've never even *known* someone with a credit card before."

I had only recently acquired my credit card while looking for Aahz on Perv, and hadn't had a chance to use it yet. (Frankly, except for a few dimension travelers like my colleagues and me, I don't think anyone on my home dimension of Klah has even *heard* of a credit card. I know I hadn't until I hit Perv.) If anything, I had tended to down play it, since it seemed to upset Aahz. My partner wasn't here, though, and my impressionable date was. If nothing else over the years, I've learned to go with the flow.

"Oh, it comes in handy," I said loftily, producing the item under discussion with a flourish. "Keeps me from having to carry *too* much cash, you know."

The card disappeared from my fingertips as Cassandra seized it and gaped at it in open awe.

"A solid gold card!" she exclaimed breathlessly. "Wow! You sure know how to show a girl a good time, Tiger. Are we going to party tonight!!"

Before I could stop her, she had grabbed my hand again and plunged into the crowd, holding the card aloft like a banner.

"Excuse us! Coming through!"

The people in line who we were elbowing our way past didn't like it. A few went so far as to bare their fangs in annoyance. The card seemed to have some magik effect, though, because, after one glance, they all stepped back and cleared a passage for us . . . or, rather, for Cassandra. I just trailed along in her wake.

There was a velvet rope barring the door, and a big guy beside it whose only function seemed to be to admit people a few at a time as others left . . . that, and be intimidating. I mean, he was BIG . . . and that's coming from someone who has his own bodyguards. As soon as he spotted the card, however, he snatched the rope from the door, shoving a few of the line people back to open a path for us, and actually tried to twist his features into a smile as we swept past.

It was occurring to me that there might be more to this credit card business than I imagined. This didn't seem to be the time to ask, however, and a moment later we were in the club . . . and I lost all ability to think of anything else.

Chapter Nine

"I love the nightlife."
V. Dracula

I don't know what I had expected for the interior of a vampire nightclub, probably because it never occurred to me that I might visit one someday, but this definitely wasn't it.

First and foremost, it was bright. I don't mean bright, I mean **BRIGHT!!!**

The lighting level was so intense the glare was almost blinding, particularly coming in from the darkness outside. Even squinting, it was so bright I could barely make out the features of the room and even had to grope a bit to keep from tripping over things.

"Whatdaya think?" Cassandra shouted over the music as she clung to my arm.

"Hard to tell!" I called back. "It's kinda bright!"

"I know! Isn't it *great!*" she said, flashing a smile that shone through the light. "Real spooky, isn't it?"

For some reason, that made sense. In fact, suddenly the whole club did. Humans were primarily daylight lovers. When they wanted to feel daring or be scared, they went to dark places. Vampires, on the other hand, normally tended to shun the light. As such, I supposed it was only natural that a place lit up like a flare would be scary to them.

"Oh, it's not too bad . . . once your eyes adjust to it," I said loftily.

It was the truth. My eyes were slowly getting used to the glare, allowing me to look around the place.

What it lacked in size, it made up for in noise and customers.

What seemed like hundreds of people were packed around an expanse of tiny tables, each table having a small umbrella to provide limited relief from the bright lights like . . . well, like candles on tables in a dark room back where I came from.

The only portion that seemed even more crowded than the tables was a small space I took for a dance floor. I made this assumption based on the fact that the customers packed in there cheek to jowl were all moving rhythmically in unison to the music which was blaring through the place at a volume level to match the Big Game. I couldn't see a source for the music, unless it was from the one wierd looking guy who was ensconced behind a table overlooking the dance floor. Every so often, there would be a break in the music and he would shout something, whereupon the crowd would shout back at him and a new tune would start. From this, I guessed that he had something to do with the entertainment, but exactly what I couldn't be sure, as there was no sign of an instrument. Just stacks and stacks of shiny discs he kept feeding into a machine in front of him.

The music itself was beyond description . . . unless that description is "loud." Mostly, it sounded like jarring crashes of noise repeated endlessly to a driving beat. I mentioned that there would be pauses and new tunes, but in truth they seemed remarkably alike to me. I mean, whether one is repeatedly hitting a sackful of tin cans or a sackful of pots and kettles, or alternating between the two, the overall sound effect is the same for all intents and purposes. The crowd seemed to enjoy it, though, or, at least, it was sufficient to keep them cheering and gyrating with apparently limitless energy.

With all the noise and activity that was going on, I was almost surprised that I managed to notice the decorations hanging on the walls. Perhaps they caught my eye with their sheer incongruity.

There were strings of garlic . . . fake, to look at it . . . , as well as vials of water and strings of beads, all marked with various religious symbols. Not exactly what I'd pick to have around while I was trying to relax . . . if I were a vampire. Then again, the objective of the place didn't seem to be to provide relaxation.

"Interesting decor," I said, still looking at the stuff on the walls. "What's the name of this place, anyway?"

"It's called The Wooden Stake," Cassandra supplied, giving a mock shudder as she hugged my arm even tighter. "Isn't it a gas?"

"Uh huh," I managed noncommittally.

Actually, her little shudder was quite distracting . . . particularly crowded as close to me as she was.

"Quite a crowd here," I added, forcibly pulling my eyes away from her to look around again.

"I *told* you it was the hottest club around," she said, giving my arm a small shake. "Look. *Everybody's* here."

If it seems that I've been dwelling on the physical description of the club, it's because I've been hesitant to tackle the job of describing the patrons. They were like something out of your worse nightmare . . . literally.

As might be expected, there were vampires. If their red eyes and flashy clothes didn't give them away, there was always the minor detail that they tended to float above the dance floor and along the ceiling to get away from the crush of the other dancers.

The list didn't stop there, however.

There were 'weres' around. Not just werewolves, but were-tigers, were-bears, and were-snakes as well. There were also mummies, lizard men, a night-shambler or two, and even a couple ghosts. At least, you could see through them so I supposed they were ghosts.

Just your average, run of the mill, neighborhood bar crowd
. . . if your neighborhood happens to be the intersection of
half a dozen horror movies.

"I don't see the Woof Writers anywhere," I said, just to be
cantankerous. I didn't know many people here on Limbo, but
the few I knew weren't here, so obviously *everybody* wasn't in
attendance.

"Oh, Idnew is probably around somewhere," Cassandra said
absently, scanning the crowd. "Don't expect to see Drachir,
though. He's usually holed up somewhere quieter talking business or . . . "

She broke off suddenly and looked at me sharply.

"You know the Woof Writers?"

"Like I said," I smiled, squeezing *her* arm for a change. "I've
been on Limbo before."

"*Look! There's a table!*" She grabbed my wrist and took off
through the crowd, towing me along behind. If I had been
hoping to impress her, I'd have to work more on my timing.

We barely beat out a vampire couple for the table, who
favored us with dark glares before continuing their search. I
watched their departure with a vague sense of relief. I *really*
didn't want to get into a fight tonight . . . and *especially* not here
in the Wooden Stake. I hadn't felt so much like an outsider
since I returned from Perv.

The view from our table was notably much more restricted
than the one we had when we were standing due to the crush of
people around us. The only real advantage to having a table
that I could see, was that we didn't have to hold our drinks . . .
except we didn't have any drinks.

"What'll you have?"

For a moment, I thought the question had come telepathi-
cally in answer to my thoughts. Then I realized there was a
ghost hovering next to me, nearly translucent, but carrying a
solid enough tray. I supposed it made sense. A ghost to pass
ethereally through the crowds, and a solid tray to carry the
drinks on. Maybe if other bars and restaurants used the same

idea, service would be faster.

"Hi, Marley. I'll have a Bloody Mary," Cassandra said. "What do you want, Tiger?"

I'll spare you the image which my mind came up with to associate with the name of her ordered drink. While I knew from my earlier visits that vampires don't necessarily drink human blood exclusively, the idea of imbibing any kind of blood was pretty low on my list for taste treats.

"Um . . . What all do they have?" I stalled. "I'm pretty much just used to wine."

"Don't worry, it's a full service bar," she informed me brightly. "They've got pretty much. . . . Oh! I get it!"

She threw back her head and laughed, then gave my arm a playful slap.

"Don't get uptight, Tiger. They do have drinks for off-worlders."

Again I was relieved, but at the same time, I wasn't wild about being laughed at. I seemed to be losing ground in the "impress your date" department.

"No, I'm serious, Cassandra," I said. "I really don't have much experience drinking except for wine."

"Hey. No problem. I'll order for you."

That wasn't exactly what I had in mind, but she had turned to our waiter before I could stop her.

"Bring him a Bloody Mary, too, Marley. A regular one, not the local version," she said. "Oh, and we'll be running a tab. Here's his credit card so you can make an imprint."

The waiter accepted the card without batting an eye . . . apparently waiters are harder to impress with credit cards than doormen . . . and moved off through the crowd. And I do mean through the crowd.

Truth to tell, I had been so busy ogling the club, I had completely forgotten that Cassandra still had my card until she handed it to the waiter. Inexperienced though I was with credit cards, I was aware that losing track of one's card is not the wisest idea, and I resolved to reclaim it when the waiter brought it back.

In the meantime, there was one minor matter I wanted to take care of . . . to wit, my outfit.

As you may recall, I spent a certain amount of time choosing my ensemble for this date, but that was before I knew we were headed for Limbo. The clothes I was wearing were fine for Klah, or even Deva, but here on Limbo they were conservative to the point of looking drab. Normally, I wouldn't squander my magik on something so trivial, particularly on Limbo, but I had already scouted a strong force line directly over the club and . . . what the heck, I *was* still trying to impress my date.

At the moment, she was busy chatting with some friends of hers who had stopped by the table, so I figured now was as good a time as any. Closing my eyes, I went to work on my outfit courtesy of my good old trusty standby . . . the disguise spell.

Since I wasn't really all that dissatisfied with the outfit I was wearing, I didn't go for any radical change, just a few adjustments here and there. I deepened the neckline on both my shirt and vest to show a bit more of my chest . . . such as it was. Then I lengthened the points on my collar and added a bit more drape to the sleeves to be more in line with some of the more billowy outfits the other men in the club were wearing. As a final touch, I added a sparkley undertone to my shirt so that it would match my date's dress . . . in texture, at least.

Like I said, not much of a change. Just enough so I wouldn't look dowdy sitting in a club with flashy vampires. I couldn't see the changes myself, of course, which is one of the few drawbacks of a disguise spell, but I had enough confidence in this, one of my oldest spells, to know it was effective. I knew my date would be able to see the changes. The only question was, would she notice?

I needn't have worried.

Not that she noticed right away, mind you. Cassandra's friends had moved on, but she was still quite busy waving and calling to others in the crowd. Apparently she was quite a popular young lady. Not surprising, really.

The fun started when the waiter brought our drinks to the

81

table. Setting them them carefully in front of us, he leaned over to speak directly into my ear.

"This first round is compliments of the manager, *sir*," he said, with notably more deference than he had shown when taking the order originally. "He asked me to tell you he's honored you're visiting our club, and hopes you enjoy it enough to make it a regular stop."

"What?" I said, genuinely taken aback. "I don't understand."

"*I said, the manager . . .* " the ghost started to repeat, but I cut him off.

"No. I mean, *why* is he buying us a round of drinks?"

"He saw your name on the credit card," the ghost said, handing the item in question back to me. "I didn't recognize you on sight, myself . . . I hope you aren't offended."

"No. It's . . . no. No offense," I managed, still trying figure out what was going on.

"What was that all about?" Cassandra said, leaning close again. She had noticed my conversation with the waiter, but hadn't been able to hear the exact words over the music.

"It's nothing," I explained. "The manager just bought us a round of drinks."

"Really?" she frowned. "That's odd. They don't usually do that here . . . at least, not for the first round. I wonder who's on duty?"

She started craning her neck trying to get a clear look at the bar. While she was doing that, I turned my attention to our drinks.

They appeared innocent enough. Basically an opaque red fluid over ice cubes with some kind of greenery sticking out of it. Hers was a darker red than mine, but aside from that, they looked the same. Cautiously, I took a sip . . . and discovered, to my relief, it tasted sort of like tomato juice.

"Hey! This is pretty good," I declared. "What's in it, anyway?"

"Hmm?" Cassandra said, turning her attention to me again. "Oh. Yours is just tomato juice and vodka."

I didn't know what vodka was, but tomato juice I could handle. The first sip had reminded me how thirsty I was after all our running around, so I downed most of the glass with my next swallow.

"Hey! Take it easy, Tiger," my date admonished. "Those things can pack a wallop if you aren't used to them . . . and it can leave a stain, so don't drip any on your . . . "

She stopped in mid-sentence and stared at my outfit.

"Say. Weren't you wearing a different shirt before?"

"Oh, it's the same shirt," I said, as casually as I could. "I just changed it a little bit. I think this is more appropriate for this place, don't you?"

"But how could you . . . I get it! Magik!"

Her reaction was everything I could have hoped for . . . except she wasn't done.

"Wait a minute. You're a friend of Vic's from Klah, and you know magik . . . right?" she said, eagerly. "Do you know a magician there named the Great Skeeve?"

This *really* surprised me, but the pieces were starting to fall into place. The picture was incredible, but I managed to keep my cool.

"As a matter of fact, I know him rather well," I said with a faint smile.

"Whatdaya know!" Cassandra declared, slapping the table with her palm. "I thought Vic was just trying to impress me when he said he knew him. Tell me, what's he like?"

That one threw me.

"Vic? He's a nice enough guy. I thought you . . . "

"No, silly. I mean Skeeve! What's he like as a person?"

This was just getting better.

"Oh, he's a lot like me," I said. "I'm just surprised you've heard of him."

"You've *got* to be kidding!" she declared, rolling her eyes. "He's about the hottest thing going as far as magicians go. *Everybody's* talking about him. You know, he engineered a jailbreak right here on Limbo?"

"I think I heard about that," I admitted.

"And just a while back, he got barred from the Dimension of Perv. Can you believe that? Perv?"

"It was a bum rap," I grimaced.

"So you really *do* know him! Come on, tell me more. When you say he's like you, do you mean he's young or what?"

As much fun as this was, I figured it was time to stop before it got out of hand.

"Cassandra," I said, carefully. "Watch my lips. He's a *lot* like me. Get it?"

She frowned, then shook her head.

"No. I don't. You make it sound like you're twins or something. Either that, or . . . "

She suddenly stared at me, her eye's widening.

"Oh, *no*," she gasped. "You don't mean you're . . . "

I held my credit card up in front of her so she could read the name on it, then favored her with my widest smile.

"Oh no! " she shrieked, loud enough to draw attention from the neighboring tables. "*You're him!!!* Why didn't you *tell* me!!"

"You never asked," I shrugged. "Actually, I thought that Vic . . . "

But by that time, I was speaking to her back . . . or, to be more specific, her rump. She was on her feet calling triumphantly to the other patrons.

"*Hey, everybody! You know who this is? This is SKEEVE THE GREAT!!!*"

Now, at different times, various people have tried to tell me that I was building a rep through the dimensions. Most recently, Bunny had brought it up when explaining how she set the prices for the services of M.Y.T.H. Inc. I guess I was sort of aware of it, and had even kind of accepted it, but for the most part I didn't really see where it made any difference in my normal day to day life. Sitting in the Wooden Stake in the dimension of Limbo, however, was not part of my normal day to day life . . . and neither was the reaction of the crowd when it learned who I was.

At first, heads turned, then drew together in whispered conversation as the whole room stared at me as if I had grown another head.

"I hope I didn't embarrass you, Skeeve . . . can I call you Skeeve? . . . but I'm just *so* excited." Cassandra was back in her seat, focusing all her attention on me. "Imagine, me out on a date with *the Great Skeeve!*"

"Umm . . . that's all right, Cassandra," I assured her, but now my attention was elsewhere.

Over her shoulder . . . heck, from all around us . . . I could see people starting to make their way toward our table. Now, as I've mentioned, I've been chased by mobs before, but never starting surrounded! Still, they didn't look particularly hostile or angry. If anything, they all seemed to have exaggerated smiles on their faces . . . which considering the array of teeth in the room, wasn't all that pleasant to behold.

"Excuse me, Cassandra," I said, eyeing the incoming people, "but I drink . . . I mean, I think we're about to have company."

The slip of the tongue was because I had just tried to take another sip of my drink, only to find the glass was empty except for the ice cubes . . . strange, because I didn't remember finishing it. Then the first person reached the table.

It was a male vampire, all decked out in a fine set of evening clothes which he wore with enviable grace.

"Excuse me for interrupting, Mr. Skeeve," the he said with a smile, "but I wanted to shake your hand. Always wanted to meet you, but never thought I'd get the opportunity."

"Uh, sure," I said, but he had already seized my hand and was pumping away.

"I was wondering . . . could I have your autograph?" a young lady said, trying to edge around the first gentleman.

"What? I suppose so . . . "

Unfortunately I couldn't seem to get my hand loose from the vampire who was still shaking it, though he seemed to be looking elsewhere at the moment.

"Hey! Waiter!" I heard him call. "Another round of whatever

Mr. Skeeve and his guest are drinking . . . and put it on my tab!"

"Umm . . . thank you," I said, extracting my hand, and turning to the girl who had asked for an autograph. "Do you have a pen?"

"Gosh no!" she exclaimed. "But I'll go get one. Don't go away, I'll be right back."

I really didn't know what to think. I had been nervous about coming back to Limbo because of my near criminal activities during my last visit, and here they were treating me like a celebrity!

"Mr. Skeeve. If you don't mind. It's for my little girl."

This last was from a were-tiger who thrust both paper and pen at me. Fortunately, after the last visitor, I knew what he was after, and hastily scribbled my signature on the page.

Our ghost waiter materialized though the growing crowd and set our drinks on the table . . . except there were three of them! From the color, one for Cassandra, and two for me.

"What's with the extra?" I said.

"Compliments of the table over there, sir," the waiter said, pointing somewhere off to my left.

I tried to look where he was indicating, and almost put my nose in the navel of another young lady who was crowding up beside me. Actually, she was one of three, any one of whom would be eye-catching under normal circumstances, but were just part of the crowd here.

"Where are you going from here, Mr. Skeeve?" the taller one purred. "There's going to be a party at our place later if you want to come by."

"Wipe your chin, Sweetheart," Cassandra smiled, slipping her arm around my shoulder. "He's *my* date . . . and I plan to keep him busy all night."

That had an intriguing sound to it, but just then someone else started tugging on my sleeve.

"Excuse me, Mr. Skeeve," said an awesome set of teeth from a point too close to focus on. "I was wondering if I might interview you sometime at your convenience?"

88

"Well . . . I'm kind of busy right now," I hedged, trying to lean back far enough to get a better look at my questioned . . . which unfortunately pressed the back of my head up against one of the party girls.

"Oh, I don't mean *now*," the teeth said, matching my retreat with a move forward so I *still* couldn't see what who was talking. "If you can stop by our table over there later, we'll set up an appointment. I'll have a drink waiting for you . . . Bloody Mary, right?"

"Right. I mean, okay. But . . . "

But by that time the person was gone. I only hoped that they'd recognize me if I got into the general vicinity. Right now, my attention was caught by the fact that whoever I was pressing backward against was now pressing forward against the back of my head . . . far too insistently for it to be an accident.

"Say, Skeeve," Cassandra said, giving me an excuse to break contact which I took, pausing only to take a gulp of my drink before I leaned toward her.

"Yes, Cassandra?"

"If you don't mind, can we head out of here after you finish your drink? There are a couple other places I'd like to hit tonight . . . you know, to show you off a little?"

"No problem," I said, "but it might take a while."

Somehow, during the last flurry of discussions, my two drinks had multiplied into four.

"Oh, I'm in no hurry," she said, giving me a quick kiss. "I know you've got to deal with some of these people now that they know who you are. It goes with the notoriety. It may be old hat to you, but I'm having a blast!"

To say the least, it wasn't old hat to me. Maybe if it was, I would have handled it better.

I remember signing my name a lot . . . and some more drinks being delivered . . . and kissing Cassandra . . . and, I think, another club . . . or two other clubs . . . and more drinks . . .

Chapter Ten

"Happiness is defined by one's capacity for enjoyment."
Bacchus

O pening my eyes, I suffered a brief moment of disorientation, then things started swimming into focus.

I was in my room . . . in my own bed, to be specific, though the covers seemed to be twisted and disheveled. I was naked under the covers, though I had no recollection of getting undressed. I assumed it was morning, as there was sunlight streaming though the window. In short everything looked normal.

So why did I feel there was something wrong?

I was lying on my side, and I realized my sinuses had flooded, making it impossible to breathe out of the nostril on the "downhill" side. In an effort to alleviate this situation, I rolled over and . . .

It hit me!!!

A pounding headache . . . a nauseous stomach . . . the works!

There had been times in the past when I had gotten sick, but nothing like this! At first I was afraid I was going to die. Then I was afraid I'd live. Misery such as I was feeling should have a finite end.

Groaning slightly and burrowing into my pillow, I tried to gather my thoughts.

What was going on here? What happened to make me feel . . .

Suddenly, the memory of the previous night flashed across my mind . . . or, at least, the beginning of it.

The blind date . . . the Wooden Stake . . . the admiring crowds . . . *Cassandra!*

I sat bolt upright and . . .

Big mistake. *BIG* mistake.

Every pain and queasiness I had been feeling slammed into me threefold. With a moan, I fell limply back onto my pillow heedless of the new unpleasant sensations this move caused. You could only feel so miserable, and I had bottomed out. Nothing could make me feel worse. Forget any effort at rational thought. I was just going to lie there until my head cleared or I died . . . whichever came first.

A knock sounded at the door.

Disoriented as I was, I had no difficulty deciding what to do: I was going to ignore it. I was certainly in no condition to see or talk to anyone!

The knock came again, a little louder this time.

"Skeeve? Are you awake?"

It was Bunny's voice. From what I could recall of the begin-ning of last evening, I *really* didn't want to talk to her right now. All I needed to make my misery complete was to have her carping on me about my taste in dates.

"Go away!" I called, not even bothering to try to make it sound polite.

As soon as I uttered the words, however, I realized I would have been better off just staying quiet. Not only had the effort increased the pounding in my head, I had inadvertently let her know I was awake.

As if in response to my afterthought, the door opened and Bunny came in, a big tray of food in her hands.

"When I didn't see you at breakfast *or* at lunch, I figured you

might be a little worse for wear from last night," she said crisply, setting the tray on my desk. "I had the kitchen put together a tray for you to help you back to the land of the living."

Food was definitely low on my list of priorities at the moment. If anything, I was more concerned with things going the other way through my digestive tract. It *did* however, suddenly occur to me that I was thirsty. In fact, VERY thirsty.

"Have you got any juice on that tray?" I managed weakly, not wanting to sit up far enough to look myself.

"Do you want orange or tomato?"

The mention of tomato juice brought memories of last night's Bloody Marys to mind, and my stomach did a slow roll and dip to the left.

"Orange will be fine," I said through gritted teeth, trying hard to talk, keep my mouth shut, and swallow at the same time.

She favored me with a speculative glance.

"Well, it wasn't Screwdrivers or Mimosas."

"Excuse me?"

"Never mind. Orange juice, coming up."

I could have done without the "coming up" comment, but the juice tasted fine. I downed it in two long swallows. Strangely enough, it left me even more thirsty. Not that the juice wasn't a welcome input of cool moisture, but it made me realize just how dehydrated I was.

"Any more of that?" I said hopefully.

"Got a whole pitcher here," Bunny replied, gesturing toward the tray. "I had a hunch you were going to need more than one glass. Take it slow, though. I don't think it would be a good idea to gulp down a lot of cold liquid just yet."

I resisted the urge to grab the entire pitcher from her, and instead simply held out my glass for a refill. With a major effort, I did my best to comply with her suggestion and sipped it slowly. It lasted a little longer that way, and did seem to have a greater effect.

"That's better," she said, refilling the glass again without being asked. "So. Did you have a good time last night?"

I paused in mid-sip, trying to force my brain to function.

"To be honest with you, Bunny, I don't know," I admitted at last.

"I'm not sure I follow you."

"What I remember was okay," I said, "but after a certain point in the evening, everything's a blank. I'm not even sure exactly when that point was, for that matter. Things are a bit jumbled in my mind still.

"I see."

For a moment, Bunny seemed about to say something else, but instead she pursed her lips and wandered over to the widow where she stood staring out.

My head was clearing now, to a point where I felt almost alive, and I decided it was time to try to set things right.

"Um . . . Bunny? About last night . . . I'm sorry I left you standing like that, but Vic had set up the date for me, and there was no real way to back out gracefully."

"Of course, the fact that she was quite a dish had nothing to do with it," Bunny commented with a grimace.

"Well . . . "

"Don't worry about it, Skeeve," she said quickly, waving off my reply. "That's not what's bothering me, anyway."

"What is?"

She turned to face me, leaning back on the window sill.

"It's the same thing that's been bothering me ever since I arrived for this assignment," she said. "I haven't wanted to say anything, because it's really none of my business. But if what you say about last night is true . . . "

She broke off, biting her lip slightly.

"Go on," I said.

"Well . . . Simply put, I think you're developing a drinking problem."

That one caught me off guard. I had been half expecting her to make some comment about how little I was helping on the kingdom's finances, or even the parade of women I seemed to be suddenly confronted with. It had never occurred to me that she might be taking affront at my personal habits.

"I . . . I don't know what to say, Bunny. I mean, sure, I drink. But everybody drinks a little from time to time."

"A *little?*"

She came off the window sill in one easy motion and came to perch on the edge of my bed.

"Skeeve, every time I see you lately you've got a goblet of wine in your hand. It's gotten so that your idea of saying 'Hello' to someone is to offer them a drink."

I was really confused now. When she first mentioned my drinking, my immediate reaction was that she was being an alarmist. The more she talked, however, the more I found myself wondering if she might have a point.

"That's just being hospitable," I said, stalling for time to think.

"Not when you're making the offer first thing in the morning," she snapped. "Definitely not when you go ahead and have a drink yourself, whether they join you or not."

"Aahz drinks," I countered, starting to feel defensive. "He says the water on most dimensions isn't to be trusted."

"This is your home dimension, Skeeve. You should be used to the water here. Besides, Aahz is a Pervect. His whole metabolism is different from yours. He can handle drinking."

"And I can't. Is that what you're trying to say?"

The misery I had been feeling since I awoke was now taking the form of anger and annoyance.

"Check me on this," she said. "From what I've heard, during your recent trip to Perv, you got into a fight didn't you? After you'd been drinking?"

"Well . . . Yes. But I've been in fights before."

"From what I hear, if Kalvin, the Djinn, hadn't sobered you up, you might not have survived this one. True?"

She had a point there. The situation *had* been a bit hairy. I had to admit that my odds of surviving the brawl would have gone way down if I hadn't been jerked back to sobriety by Kalvin's spell.

I nodded my agreement.

"Then there's last night," she continued. "You really wanted to make a good impression on someone. You dressed up in one of your spiffiest outfits, probably dropped a fair hunk of change, and then what? From the sounds of it, you got carried away with the drinking until you can't even remember what happened. You don't even know what went on, much less whether or not your date had a good time. That doesn't sound like you . . . at least, the you that you'd like people to remember."

I was starting to feel really low, and not just from the after effects of the night before. I had always thought my drinking was a harmless diversion . . . or, more lately, a way to ease the pressures of the problems confronting me. It had never occurred to me how it might look to others. Now that I was thinking about it, the picture wasn't very pleasant. Unfortunately, I was still a little reluctant to admit that to Bunny."

One of the things I *do* remember about last night is that people kept buying me drinks," I said defensively. "It kind of caught me by surprise, and I thought it would be rude to refuse."

"Even if you *have* to accept drinks to be social, there's nothing that says that what you drink has to be alcoholic," Bunny shot back. "There *are* other things to drink, you know. You could always just have a soft drink or some fruit juice."

Suddenly, I was very tired. Between my hangover and the new thoughts that had been thrust upon me, what little energy I had when I awoke was now depleted.

"Bunny," I said, "I'm really not up to arguing with you right now. You've raised some interesting points, and I appreciate your bringing them to my attention. Give me some time to think about them. Okay? At the moment, all I want to do is curl up and die for a while."

To her credit, Bunny didn't continue to push her case. Instead, she became extremely solicitous.

"I'm sorry, Skeeve," she said, laying a hand on my arm. "I didn't mean to jump you like that while you were still drying out. Is there anything I can get you? A cold washrag, maybe?"

Actually, that sounded like a wonderful idea.

"If you would, please. I'd really appreciate it."

She hopped off the bed and made for the washstand while I tried to find a more comfortable position.

After rearranging the pillows, I glanced over to see what was keeping her, only to find her standing stock still, staring at the wall.

"Bunny? Is there something wrong?" I called.

"I guess I was wrong," she said in a strange tone, still staring at the wall.

How's that?"

"When I said you probably left a bad impression on you date . . . I think I should have kept my mouth shut."

"What makes you say that?"

"I take it you haven't seen this."

She gestured at the wall over the washstand. I squinted slightly and focused my still bleary eyes on the spot she was indicating.

Written on the wall, in bright red lipstick, was a note.

Skeeve,
Sorry to go, but I didn't want to wake you.
Last night was magic. You're as good as your rep.
Let me know when you want to play some more.
                                                    Cassandra

I found myself smirking slightly as I read the note.

"Well, I guess she wasn't too upset with my drinking. Eh, Bunny?"

There was no answer.

"Bunny?"

I tore my eyes away from the message and glanced around the room. The tray was still there, but Bunny wasn't. With the door standing open, the only logical conclusion was that she had left without saying a word.

Suddenly, I didn't feel so smug anymore.

Chapter Eleven

"If labor and management communicated better,
there would be fewer terminations"
J. Hoffa

"**H**i, Buttercup. How's it going, fellah?"

The war unicorn raised his head and stared at me for a moment, then went back to eating from his feed bin.

"Com'on, fellah. You know me," I urged.

The unicorn continued eating, ignoring me completely.

"Don't worry, Boss," came a squeaky voice from behind me. "Unicorns are like that."

I didn't have to look to see who the voice belonged to, but turned to face my bodyguard anyway.

"Hi, Nunzio," I said. "What was that about unicorns?"

"They're temperamental," he explained with a shrug. "War unicorns like Buttercup are no exception. He's just giving you a rough time because you haven't been visiting him much."

One of the assorted things I had learned about Nunzio's past was that at one time he had been an animal trainer, so I tended to believe him. I was a little disappointed, however. I had been hoping that Buttercup's reaction to me would provide a confirmation as to what did or didn't happen between Cassandra and me the night before, but it seemed there were other, more rational, possible reasons for his standoffishness.

Of course, fast on the heels of my disappointment came a surge of guilt. I *had* been neglecting my pets badly . . . along with a lot of other things.

"That reminds me, Nunzio," I said, eager to shift the guilt, "how are you doing with Gleep?"

My bodyguard frowned and wiped a massive hand across his mouth and chin in thought.

"I dunno, Boss," he said. "I can't quite put my finger on it, but there's somethin' wrong there. He just don't *feel* right lately."

Strangely enough, that made sense. In fact, Nunzio had managed to put into words my own nebulous concerns about my pet . . . he didn't *feel* right.

"Maybe we're going about this wrong," I said. "Maybe instead of trying to pin down what's wrong with him *now*, we should try to backtrack a bit."

"I don't quite follow you," my bodyguard scowled.

"Think back, Nunzio," I urged. When did you first notice that Gleep wasn't acting normal?"

"Well . . . he seemed okay when Markie was around," He said thoughtfully. "In fact, if you think about it, he was the first of us to figure she wasn't on the up and up."

Something flitted across my mind along with that memory, but Nunzio kept talking and it disappeared again.

"I'd have to say it was right after that job when him and me was guarding that warehouse. You remember? With the forged comic books?"

"Was he all right on that assignment?"

"Sure. I remember talkin' with him quite a bit while we was sittin' around doin' nothin'. He was fine then."

"Wait a minute," I interrupted. "You were talking *with* Gleep?"

"I guess it was more like talkin' *to* him, since he doesn't really answer back." Nunzio corrected himself easily. "You know what

I mean, Boss. Anyway, I spent a lot of time talkin' *to* him, and he seemed okay then. In fact, he seemed to listen real close."

"What did you talk to him about?"

My bodyguard hesitated, then glanced away quickly.

"Oh . . . this and that," he said with an exaggerated shrug. "I really can't remember for sure."

"Nunzio," I said, letting a note of sternness creep into my voice, "if you can remember, tell me. It's important."

"Well . . . I was goin' on a bit about how worried I was about you, Boss," Nunzio admitted hesitantly. "You remember how you was right after we decided to incorporate? How you was gettin' so wrapped up in work that you didn't have much time for anything or anyone else? I just unloaded on Gleep a bit about how I didn't think it was healthy for you, is all. I didn't think it would hurt nothin'. That's why I did my talkin' in front of him and not anyone else on the team . . . even Guido."

There were clear images dancing in my head now. Pictures of Gleep breathing fire at Markie . . . who only escaped narrowly when Nunzio intervened . . . and of my pet throwing himself in front of me when another, larger dragon was on the brink of making me extinct.

"Think carefully, Nunzio," I said slowly. "When you were talking to Gleep, did you say anything . . . anything at all . . . about the possibility of Tananda or anyone else on the team being a threat to me?"

My bodyguard frowned thoughtfully for a moment, then shook his head.

"I don't remember sayin' anything like that, Boss. Why do you ask?"

Now it was my turn to hesitate. The idea that was taking shape in my mind seemed almost too silly to voice. Still, since I was turning to Nunzio for advice and expertise, it was only fair to share my suspicions with him.

"It may be crazy," I said, "but I'm starting to get the feeling that Gleep is a lot more intelligent that we ever suspected. I mean, he's always been kind of protective of me. If he *were* intelligent and got it into his head that someone on the team was a threat to me, there's a chance he might try to kill them . . . just like he went after Markie."

My bodyguard stared at me, then gave a short bark of laughter.

"You're right, Boss," he said. "That *does* sound crazy. I mean, Gleep's a dragon! If he was to try to whack someone on the team, we'd know it pretty fast, know what I mean?"

"Like when he tried to burn Tananda?" I pressed. "Think about it, Nunzio. If he *were* intelligent, wouldn't part of his conclusions be that I would be upset if anything happened to anyone on the team? In that case, wouldn't he do his best to make any mishap look like an accident rather than a direct attack? I'll admit it's a wild theory, but it fits the facts."

"Except for one thing," my bodyguard countered. "For him to be doin' what you say, puttin' pieces together and comin' up with his own conclusions, much less organizing a plan and executing it, would make him more than intelligent. It would make him smarter than us! Remember, for a dragon he's still real young. It would be like sayin' a baby that could hardly walk was planning a bank heist."

"I suppose you're right," I sighed. "There must be another explanation."

"You know, Boss," Nunzio smiled, "folks say that, after a while, pets start takin' on the traits of their masters and vice verses. Takin' that into consideration, I think it's only logical that Gleep here acts a bit strange from time to time."

For some reason, that brought to mind my earlier conversation with Bunny.

"Tell me, Nunzio, do you think I've been drinking too much lately?"

"That's not for me to say, Boss," he said easily. "I'm just a bodyguard, not a babysitter."

"I was asking what you thought."

"And I'm sayin' I'm not supposed to think . . . at least, not about whoever it is I'm supposed to be guardin'," he insisted.

101

"Bodyguards what comment on their client's personal habits don't last long. What I'm supposed to be doin' is guardin' you while you do whatever it is you do . . . not tellin' you what to do."

I started to snap at him, but instead took a long breath and brought my irritation under control.

"Look, Nunzio," I said carefully, "I know that's the normal bodyguard/client relationship. I like to think, though, that we've progressed a little past that point. I like to think of you as a friend as well as a bodyguard. What's more, you're a stockholder in M.Y.T.H. Inc., so you have a vested interest in my performance as president. Now, this morning Bunny told me that she thought I was developing a drinking problem. I don't think that I am, but I'm aware that I may be too close to the situation to judge properly. That's why I'm asking your opinion . . . as a friend and fellow worker whose opinions and judgment I've grown to value and respect."

Nunzio rubbed his chin thoughtfully, obviously wrestling with a mental dilemma.

"I dunno, Boss," he said. "It's kinda against the rules . . . but then again you're right. You do treat Guido and me different from any other boss we've had. Nobody else ever asked our opinion on nothin'."

"Well I'm asking, Nunzio. Please?"

"Part of the problem is that it's not that easy a question to answer," he shrugged. "Sure, you drink. But do you drink too much? That's not as clear cut. You've been drinking more since you brought Aahz back from Perv, but 'more' doesn't necessarily mean the same as 'too much.' Know what I mean?"

"As a matter of fact, no I don't."

He sighed heavily. When he spoke again, I couldn't help but notice that his tone had the patient, careful note that one takes, or should, when one is explaining something to a child.

"Look, Boss," he said. "Drinkin' affects the judgment. Everybody knows that. The more you drink, the more it affects your judgment. Sayin' how much is too much isn't easy, though, seein' as how it varies from individual to individual depending on such factors as weight, temperament, etc."

"But if it affects your judgment," I said, "how can you tell whether or not your judgment is right when you say it's not too much?"

"That's the rub," Nunzio shrugged. "Some say if you have the sense to question it, you aren't drinkin' too much. Others say that if you have to ask, then you ARE drinkin' too much. One thing I do know is that a lot of people who drink too much are sure they don't have a problem."

"So how do you tell?"

"Well," he said, rubbing his chin, "probably the best way is to ask a friend whose judgment you trust."

I closed my eyes and fought for patience.

"That's what I THOUGHT I was doing, Nunzio. I'm asking YOU. Do YOU think I'm drinking too much?"

"That isn't important," he said, blandly. "It isn't a question of if I think you're drinkin' too much, it's if YOU think you're drinkin' too much."

"NUNZIO," I said through gritted teeth. "I'm asking what YOUR opinion is."

He averted his eyes and shifted uncomfortably.

"Sorry, Boss. Like I say, this isn't easy for me."

He rubbed his chin again.

"One thing I WILL say is that I think you're drinkin' at the wrong time . . . and I don't mean too early or late in the day. I mean at the wrong time in your life."

"I don't understand," I frowned.

"Ya see, Boss, drinkin' usually acts like a magnifyin' glass. It exaggerates everything. Some people drink tryin' to change their mood, but they're kiddin' themselves. It don't work that way. It don't change what is, it emphasizes it. If you drink when you're happy, then you get REAL happy. Know what I mean? But if you drink when you're down, then you get REAL down, REAL fast."

He gave another heavy sigh.

"Now, you've been goin' through some rough times lately,

and have some tough decisions to make. To me, that's not a real good time to be drinkin'. What you need right now is a clear head. What you DON'T need is somethin' to exaggerate any doubts you've got about yourself or your judgment."

It was my turn to rub my chin thoughtfully.

"That makes sense," I said. "Thanks, Nunzio."

"Hey. I just had an idea," he said brightly, apparently buoyed by his success. "There's a real easy way to tell if you're drinkin' too much. Just lay off the sauce for a while. Then see if there's any big change in your thinkin' or judgment. If there is, then you know it's time to back off. Of course, if you find out that quittin' is harder than you thought, then you'll have another signal that you've got trouble."

A part of me bristled at the thought of having to ease up on my drinking, but I fought it down . . . along with my flash fear at what that bristling might imply.

"Okay, Nunzio," I said. "I'll do it. Thanks again. I appreciate how hard that was for you."

"Don't mention it, Boss. Glad I could help you."

He reached out and laid a hand on my shoulder in a rare display of comradeship.

"Personally, I don't think you have that much to worry about. If you've got a drinkin' problem, it's marginal at best. I mean, it's not like you've been blackin' out or anything."

Chapter Twelve

"Let's see the instant replay on that!"
H. Cossell

"**H**ey, Partner! How's it going?"

I had been heading back toward my room with the vague thought of getting a little more sleep. The hail from Aahz, however, reduced my odds of success noticeably.

"Hi Aahz," I said, turning toward him. That put the sun in my eyes, so I stepped back slightly to find some shade.

He drew up close to me and peered at me carefully. I, in turn, tried my best to look relaxed and puzzled.

Finally he nodded to himself.

"You look okay," he declared.

"Shouldn't I?" I said, innocently.

"I heard you had quite a time last night," he explained, shooting me another sidelong glance. "Thought I'd better look you up and survey the damage. I'll admit you seem to have weathered the storm well enough. Resilience of youth, I guess."

"Maybe the reports were exaggerated," I suggested hopefully.

"Not bloody likely," he snorted. "Chumley said he saw you and your date when you rolled back into the castle, and as you know, if anything he's prone to understatement."

I nodded mutely. When he wasn't in his working persona of Big Crunch, the troll was remarkably accurate in his reports and observations.

"Whatever," Aahz waved. "Like I say, you seem to have survived pretty well."

I managed a weak smile.

"How about a hair of the dog? A quick drink to perk you up," he suggested. "Com'on partner. My treat. We'll duck into town for a change of pace."

A moment's reflection was all it took to realize that a stroll through the town around the castle sounded good. Real good if Bunny was on the warpath.

"Okay, Aahz. You're on," I said. "But as to the Hair of the Dog . . . I'll stick to regular stuff if you don't mind. I had enough of strange drinks last night."

He gave off one of those choking noises he used to make during my days as an apprentice when I said something really dumb, but when I glanced at him, there wasn't a trace of a smile.

"Aren't you forgetting something, partner?" he said without looking at me.

"What?"

"If we're heading out among the common folk, a disguise spell would be nice."

He was right of course. Even though I was used to seeing him as he actually was, a Pervect with green scales and yellow eyes, the average citizen of Possiltum still tended to react to his appearance with horror and fear . . . which is to say much the same way I reacted when I first met him.

"Sorry, Aahz."

Closing my eyes, I quickly made the necessary adjustments. Manipulating his image with my mind, I made him look like an ordinary castle guard. If anything, I made him a bit more scrawny and undernourished than average. I mean, the idea *was* not to intimidate people, wasn't it?

Aahz didn't even bother checking his reflection in any of the windows we passed. He seemed much more interested in prying details of my date out of me.

"Where did you find to go on this backwater dimension, anyway?" he said.

"Oh, we didn't stick around here," I said loftily. "We ducked over to Limbo. Cassandra knew a couple clubs there and we . . . "

I suddenly noticed Aahz was no longer walking beside me. Looking back, I realized he had stopped in his tracks. His mouth was working, but no sound came out.

"Limbo?" he managed at last. "You went bar crawling on Limbo? Excuse me, partner, but I was under the impression we were *persona non grata* in that neck of the woods."

"I was a little worried at first," I admitted casually, which was only a little lie. As you'll recall, I had been a LOT worried. "Cassandra said she could blip us back out fast if there was any trouble, though, so I figured what the heck. As it turned out, nobody seems to be holding a grudge there. In fact, it seems I'm . . . I mean, *we're* . . . minor celebrities over there. That's partly why the evening ran as long as it did. Half the people we ran into wanted to buy me a drink for putting one over on the local council."

"Is that a fact?" Aahz said darkly, starting to move again. "Just who is this Cassandra person, anyway? She doesn't exactly sound like a local."

"She's not," I confirmed. "Vic set me up with her. She's a friend of his."

"Nice to know he didn't set you up with an enemy," my partner quipped. Still in all, it seems to me . . . "

He broke off and did another double take.

"Wait a minute. Vic? The same vampire Vic that you hang around with over at the Bazaar? You mean this Cassandra babe is . . . "

"A vampire," I said with a careless shrug. The truth was, I was starting to get a bit of a kick out of shocking Aahz. "Oh, she's okay. No one you'd want to take home to mother, but . . . what's wrong?"

He was craning his neck around to peer at my neck from different angles.

"Just checking for bite marks," he said.

"Com'on, Aahz. There wasn't any danger of that. She was drinking her blood out of a glass last night."

"Those weren't the kind of bite marks I was checking for," he grinned. "Vamps have a rep of being pretty wild women."

"Um . . . speaking of destinations," I said eager to change the subject, "where are *we* going?"

"No place special," my partner said. "These local bars and inns are pretty much all the same. This one should do us fine."

With that, he veered through the door of the place we were passing, leaving me to follow along behind.

The inn was refreshingly ordinary compared to what I could remember of the surreal clubs I had been to on Limbo. Ordinary, and more than a little dull.

Dark wooden tables and chairs were the main feature of the decor, with occasional candles scattered here and there to supplement the light which streamed in through windows and the open door.

"What'll you have, Skeeve?" Aahz called, heading for the bar.

I started to say 'Wine,' but changed my mind. Whether or not Bunny was right about my drinking getting out of hand, it wouldn't hurt to ease up a bit. Besides, Nunzio's comment about blacking out had me more than a little uneasy.

"Just some fruit juice for me," I waved.

Aahz paused, cocking his head at me.

"Are you sure you're all right, partner?" he said.

"Sure. Why do you ask?"

"A while back you were talking about looking forward to having your usual, and now you're switching drinks."

"All right. Have it your way," I grimaced. "A goblet of wine, then. No need to make a big thing of it."

I leaned back and looked around the room, though it was mostly to break eye contact with Aahz before he realized I was upset. It was funny, but I found myself somehow reluctant to tell my partner my worries about my drinking. Still, it was difficult to change my drinking patterns around him without raising questions that would require an explanation. I figured that, for the moment, the easiest thing to do would be to go on as before . . . at least, while I was around Aahz. Later, more privately, I'd start tapering off.

One thing I noticed about the inn was that there seemed to be a lot of young people hanging around. Well, to be honest, they were about my age, but I spend so much time with the team, I tend to think of myself as older.

One table of girls in particular caught my attention, mostly because they seemed to be talking about me. At least, that was my guess, as they kept glancing my way, then putting their heads together and giggling, then glancing over again.

Not long ago, this would have made me nervous. My recent excursion to Limbo, however, had gotten me a bit more used to notoriety.

The next time they glanced over, I looked directly back at them, then gave a brief, polite nod of acknowledgment with my head. This, of course, caused another hurried huddle and burst of giggles.

Ah, fame.

"What are you smiling at?" Aahz said as he set my wine in front of me and slid onto the bench across the table, cradling his own outsized drink.

"Oh, nothing," I smiled. "I was just watching that table of girls over there."

I indicated the direction with a tilt of my head, and he leaned sideways to scope them out himself.

"Kind of young for you, aren't they, partner?"

"They're not that much younger than I am," I protested, taking a long swallow of wine.

"Don't you have enough problems already?" Aahz said, settling back. "Last time I checked, you were suffering from an overabundance of women . . . not a shortage."

"Oh, relax," I laughed. "I wasn't figuring to *do* anything with them. Just having a little fun, is all. They were looking at me, so I let them see me looking back."

"Well don't look now," he grinned back, "but at least one of them is doing more than looking."

Needless to say, I looked.

One of the girls had stood up and was approaching our table. When she saw me looking in her direction, she seemed to gather her courage and closed the distance in a rush.

"Hi," she said, brightly. "You're him, aren't you? The wizard from the castle?"

"That's right," I nodded. "How did you know that?"

"I thought I heard him call you Skeeve when he went to fetch your drink." she gushed.

"Probably because that's my name," I smiled.

Okay, so it wasn't the wittiest thing I've said. In fact, it was pretty lame compared to the usual banter that goes on within the team. You'd never tell it, though, from her reaction.

She covered her mouth with one hand and shrieked with laughter loud enough to draw the attention of everyone in the room . . . in the town, for that matter.

"Oh! That's *priceless*," she declared.

"That's where you're wrong," I corrected. "Actually, my rates are rather high."

This, of course, set of another gale of laughter. I caught Aahz's gaze and winked. He rolled his eyes in disgust and turned his attention to his drink. That seemed like a good idea, but when I went to sip my wine, the goblet was empty. I started to ask Aahz to get me another, but changed my mind. That first one had disappeared with disturbing speed.

"So, what can I do for you?" I said, as much to take my mind off the wine as to get an answer.

"Well, everyone in town has been talking about you," the girl chirped, "and my girlfriend . . . the cute one over there . . . has a *real* thing for you since she saw you in court when you first came back. Anyway, it would just make her whole incarnation if you'd come over to our table so she could meet you personally."

"I don't know," I said. "There are things to be said for meeting people im-personally as well."

"Huh?" she said, giving me a blank look, and I realized I had pushed beyond her sense of humor.

"Just tell her I'll be over in a few moments, as soon as I finish my conversation here."

"Great! She'll *die!* "

I watched her scamper off to tell her friends, then turned back to Aahz.

"I *may* throw up," he announced.

"You're just jealous," I grinned. "Keep and eye on my drink for me, will you?"

With that I rose and headed for the girls' table. At least, I started to.

There was a gangly youth blocking my way. I started to move around him, but he stepped sideways, deliberately putting himself in my path again.

I stopped and looked at him.

I'd been in fights before. Sometimes against some pretty tough customers when I wasn't sure I would survive it. This joker, however, was different.

He couldn't have been more than my age. Probably a few years younger. What's more, he didn't hold himself with the confident poise of a brawler or even a soldier. In fact, if anything, he looked scared.

"Leave them alone," he said in a shaky voice.

"I beg your pardon?"

"I said leave them alone!" he repeated, his voice gaining a bit of strength.

I let the ghost of a smile play across my face.

"Young man," I said gently, "do you know who I am?"

"Oh, I know all right," he nodded. "You're Skeeve. The big bad wizard from the castle. What's more, I know you can make me sorry I ever breathed, much less got in your way. You can turn me into a toad or make my hair burst into flame, or even

111

whistle up some nasty creature to tear me apart if you don't want to get your own hands dirty. You can squash me or anyone else you want just to get your way . . . but it doesn't make it right. Maybe it's about time someone stood up to you even if it means getting killed just for trying."

I couldn't help but notice there were some nods and mutterings of support for the youth at the other tables in the inn, and no few dark looks cast in my direction.

"All right," I said levelly. "You're standing up to me. Now make your point."

"The point is you can't just waltz in here and put moves on our women. What's more, if you try, you'll be sorry."

To emphasize his words, he reached out and gave me a shove that knocked me back so I had to take a step to recover my balance.

It was suddenly very quiet in the inn. The moment seemed to hang in the air as everyone tensed and waited to see what would happen next.

Blood was pounding in my ears.

I heard the bench behind me slide as Aahz started to get up, and I signaled behind me with my hand for him to stay out of it.

"I have no intention of putting any 'moves' on these women either now or in the future," I said carefully. "The young lady there came to my table and said that her friend wanted to meet me. I was about to comply. Period. That's it. It was an effort on my part to be polite. If, as it seems, it is somehow offensive to you or anyone else here, I'll forego the pleasure."

I looked past him to where the girls were watching.

"Ladies," I nodded. "Another day, perhaps."

With that, I turned on my heel and marched out of the place . . . angry and embarrassed, but confident that I had correctly handled a dubious situation.

It didn't help, however, that as I passed through the door, a shout from the youth came wafting after me.

"And don't come back!"

Chapter Thirteen

"The secret of popularity is confidence."
W. Allen

"**H**old up a minute, partner. We're still together, you know,"

I slowed my pace a bit, and Aahz caught up with me, falling in step beside me.

"If you don't mind the observation," he said, "that little scene back there seems to have gotten you a little upset."

"Shouldn't it have?" I snapped.

"Don't let it bother you," my partner said easily. "Locals always get upset with outsiders . . . especially when their women start flirting with them. It's a problem as old as the hills. Just ask any soldier or carny person. Don't take it personally."

He gave me a playful punch on the arm, but, for a change, I wasn't reassured.

"But they weren't reacting to an outsider, Aahz. They were reacting to *me*. I live here, too. What's more, they knew it. They knew who I was and that I work at the castle, but they still treated me like an outsider."

"As far as they're concerned, you are."

That one stopped me.

"How's that again?"

"Take a look at the facts, Skeeve," Aahz said, more serious now. "Even ignoring your travels through the dimensions, you aren't the same as them. Like you say, you work at the castle . . . and not as a chambermaid or a kitchen worker, either. You're one of the main advisors to the Queen, not to mention a possible consort . . . though I doubt they know that. Things you do and say on a daily basis affect everyone in this kingdom. That alone puts you on a different social . . . not to mention economic . . . level from the folks here in town."

That made me pause and think.

My new life and lifestyle had sort of grown up around me over the years. Socializing and/or clashing with kings or mayors had become pretty commonplace, though I had never stopped to consider it. Rather, I had always assumed that it sort of went with the territory when one was a magician. Then again, how many magicians had I met while I was growing up?

Aahz was right. My work with the team *had* cocooned me away from the rest of society to a point where I took things for granted. The extra-ordinary had become so ordinary to me, that I had ceased to be aware of, or even consider, how it must seem to the ordinary citizens.

I shook my head abruptly.

"No. There's more to it than that, Aahz. Those people back there didn't like *me*. "

"Uh huh," my partner nodded. "So what's your point?"

"*What's my point?*" I echoed a little shrilly. "Maybe you didn't understand me. I said . . . "

" . . . They didn't like you," Aahz finished. "So what?"

"What do you mean 'So what'?" I said. "Don't you want to be liked?"

My old mentor frowned slightly, then gave a shrug.

"I suppose it would be nice," he said. "But I really don't give it much thought."

"But . . . "

"And neither should you."

There was a levelness and firmness, almost a warning, in his tone that brought me up short.

Instead of protesting, I struggled for several moments trying to understand what he was trying to tell me, then surrendered with a shake of my head.

"I don't get it, Aahz. Doesn't everyone want to be liked?"

"Maybe at some level," my partner said. "But most people realize it's a wistful hope at best . . . like it would be nice if it only rained when we want it to. The reality is that it rains when it bloody well feels like it, and that some people aren't going to like you no matter what you do. The up side is that there are also people who will *like* you no matter what you do."

"I can't accept that," I said, shaking my head. "It's too fatalistic. If you're right, then there's no point in trying at all."

"Of course there is," Aahz snapped. "Just don't take everything to extremes. Okay? Reality always lies somewhere between the extremes. Not trying at all to have people like you is as silly as trying too much."

"Is that what I've been doing? Trying too much?"

My partner waggled his hand in front of him in a so-so gesture.

"Sometimes you drift dangerously close," he said. "I think that sometimes you let your desire to be liked get out of proportion. When that happens, it starts to warp your perception of yourself and the world."

"Could you give me an example or two?"

"Sure," he said easily. "Let's start with an easy one . . . like taxes.

Part of your job right now is to be a consultant on the taxes being levied on the citizens. Right?"

I nodded.

" . . . Except that people don't *like* to pay taxes. If they had their druthers, they would get the protection and services of the kingdom without paying a cent. Of course, they also realize that something for nothing is an unrealistic situation, so they accept the necessary evil of taxes. They accept it, but they don't like it. Because they don't *like* it, there is going to be an ongoing level of resentment and grumbling. Whatever the tax assessment is, it's too high, and whatever the level of services is, it's too low. That resentment is going to be focused on anyone involved with setting the taxes, which includes you and everyone else who works at the castle."

He shook his head.

"What I'm saying is that if you're in a position of decision making and power, such as you are now, you can forget about being *liked* by the people who are affected by your decisions. The best you can hope for is *respect*. "

"Wait a minute," I said, "are you saying that people can respect you without liking you?"

"Sure," Aahz said easily. "That one I can give you dozens of examples on. Since we're on the subject of taxes and finances, consider Grimble. You respect his skill and dedication even though you don't particularly like him as a person. Right?"

I had to admit that he was right there.

"Better still," he continued, "think back to when you and I first paired up. I was pretty rough on you with the magik lessons, and made you practice even when you didn't feel up to it. You didn't like me for drilling you constantly, but you did respect me."

"Um . . . Well, I didn't know you as well then as I do now." I said uneasily. "At the time, though, I guess I had to believe that you knew what you were doing, and that what you were putting me through was necessary for the learning process . . . whether I liked it or now."

"Precisely," Aahz nodded. "Don't feel bad. It's the normal reaction to an authority figure, whether it's a parent, a teacher, a boss, or a government representative. One doesn't always *like* what they make us do, but even in the midst of disliking being forced to do something, one can still admire and respect the fairness and expertise with which they do their job."

He shrugged easily.

"I guess that's it in a nutshell," he said. "You're a likeable young man, Skeeve, but sometimes I think you should worry less about being liked and more about being respected. If nothing else, it's a more realizable goal."

I though about what he had said for a few minutes.

"You're right, Aahz," I said finally. "Being respected *is* more important than being liked."

With that, I veered off to head in a different direction that the one we had been walking.

"Where are you going, partner?"

"I'm going to see Bunny," I called back. "There's a conversation we started this morning that I think we should finish."

I had a fair amount of time to think about what I wanted to say before I reached Bunny's room. It didn't help. When I got there, I was still as much at a loss of how to express my thoughts as when I started out.

I paused for a few moments, then rapped lightly on her door before I lost my nerve. Truth to tell, I was half hoping she was out or asleep, which would let me off my self-imposed hook.

"Who is it?"

So much for half-hopes. Maybe next time I should try a whole one.

"It's me, Bunny. Skeeve."

"What do you want?"

"I'd like to talk to you, if it's all right."

There was a silence that lasted just long enough for me to both get my hopes up, and to start seriously worrying.

"Just a minute."

As I waited, I could hear occasional sounds of metallic clanking, as if someone was moving stacks of iron plates . . . *heavy* iron plates, from the sound of it. This puzzled me, as I could think of no reason why Bunny would have metal plates in her room.

Then it occurred to me that she might have someone else in there with her.

"I can come back later, if this is a bad time," I called,

shutting my mind on trying speculate who might be in my assistant's quarters at this hour . . . and why.

In response, the door flew open, and Bunny stood framed in the doorway.

"Come on in, Skeeve," she said, rather breathlessly. "This is a surprise."

It certainly was.

Silhouetted against the light, at first I thought she was stark naked Then she turned, and I realized she was actually wearing a brightly colored outfit that was skin tight and hugged her body like it was painted on.

"Umm . . . " I said smoothly, unable to tear my eyes from her form.

"Sorry I'm such a mess," she said, grabbing up a towel and beginning to dab the sweat from her face and throat. "I was just working out."

Now, as you know, I've gotten pretty intense while working out my own problems in the past, but I've never felt the need to wear a special outfit while doing it. Then again, I've *never* worked up the kind of sweat doing it that Bunny seemed to. Whatever her problems were, they must be dillies.

"Is there anything I can do to help?" I said, genuinely concerned.

"No thanks," she smiled. "I was pretty much done when you knocked. Maybe sometime you can come in and spot for me, though."

Now she had lost me completely. Spot what? And how would spotting anything help her work things out?

"So what's up?" she said, perching on the edge of her bed.

Whatever her problems were, they didn't seem to have her particularly upset. I decided to hold off on trying to sort them out, at least, until I had settled what I came here to do.

"Basically, Bunny," I said, "I wanted to apologize to you."

"For what?" she seemed genuinely puzzled.

"For how I acted this morning . . . or whenever it was that I woke up."

"Oh that," she said, looking away. "There's no need to apologize. Everyone gets a bit out of sorts when they have a hangover."

It was nice of her to say that, but I wasn't about to let it slide.

"No, there's more to it than that, Bunny. You tried to raise some valid concerns about my health and well being, and I gave you a rough time because I wasn't ready to hear what you were saying. I guess I didn't want to hear it. With everything else I've been trying to sort out, I really didn't want one more problem to complicate things."

I paused and shook my head.

"I just wanted you to know that since then, I've been thinking about what you said. I've decided that you may be right about my having a drinking problem. I'm not sure, mind you, but there's enough doubt in my mind that I'm going to try to ease up for a while."

I sat down on the bed beside her, and put my arm around her shoulders.

"Whether you were right of not, though, I wanted to thank you for your caring and concern. That's what I *should* have said this morning instead of getting defensive."

Suddenly, she was hugging me, her face buried in my chest.

"Oh Skeeve," came her muffled voice. "I just get so worried about you. I know you're in the middle of making some rough decisions, and I try not to add to your problems. I just wish there was something more I could do to ease things for you, but it seems that when I try to help, I just make things worse for you."

Gradually, I became aware that she was crying softly, though I wasn't sure why. Also, I became *very* aware that there weren't many clothes between me and the body she was pressing against me . . . and that we were sitting on a bed . . . and . . .

I shut the door on that portion of my thoughts, vaguely ashamed of myself. Bunny was obviously upset and concerned for me. It was ignoble of me to taint the moment by entertaining thoughts of . . .

I shut the mental door again.

"Come on, Bunny," I said softly, stroking her hair with one

hand. "You *are* a big help to me. You know and I know that I'd be lost trying to straighten out the kingdom's finances without your knowledge. You've taken that whole burden on yourself."

I took her by the shoulders and held her away from me so that I could look into her eyes.

"As to doing more," I continued, "you're already trying harder which is probably wise. Like this morning when you talked to me about my drinking problem. I appreciate it . . . I really do. Some things I just have to work out for myself, though. That's the way it should be. Nobody else can or should make my decisions for me, since I'm the one who is going to have to live with the repercussions. All that you can do . . . all that anyone can do . . . to help me right now is to be patient with me. Okay?"

She nodded and wiped her eyes.

"Sorry about the waterworks," she said wryly. "Gods. The first time you come to my room, and I look like a mess."

"Now *that* is silly," I smiled, touching my finger to the end of her nose in mock severity. "You look terrific . . . like you always do. If you *don't* know that, you should."

After that, it was only natural to kiss her . . . a short, friendly kiss. At least, that's the way it started out. Then it started to last longer, and longer, and her body seemed to melt against mine.

"Well, I better say goodnight now," I said, pulling away from her. "Big day tomorrow."

That was a blatant lie, as tomorrow promised to be no more or less busy for me than any other day. I realized, however, that if I didn't break things up, and our physical involvement grew, I'd have trouble convincing myself that the reason I had come to Bunny's room was to apologize and thank her for her concern.

For a mad moment, I thought she was going to protest my leaving. If she had, I'm not sure the strength of my resolve would have been sufficient to get me out the door.

She started to say something, then stopped and drew a deep breath instead.

"Good night, Skeeve," she said finally. "Come and see me

again sometime . . . soon."

To say the least, there were many distracting thoughts dancing in my head as I made my way back to my room.

Bunny had come on to me pretty strong when we first met, and I had backed her off. Having made such a big thing out of keeping our relationship on a professional basis, could I now reverse my stance without making a complete fool of myself? Would she let me? She seemed to still be interested, but then again I might simply be kidding myself.

Then, too, there was the question of whether or not I had any right to be shopping around for a new relationship while I was still making up my mind on Queen Hemlock's proposal. The night with Cassandra had been an adventure and a learning experience, but even I couldn't kid myself that getting involved with Bunny would be a brief fling.

What was it exactly that I wanted . . . and from who?

Still lost in thought, I opened the door to my room . . . and found a demon waiting for me.

Chapter Fourteen

"Take a walk on the wild side."
G. Gebel-Williams

Now, those of you who have been following my adventures are aware that there is nothing new about my finding a demon in my room. It's not all that unusual these days, though I still have trouble from time to time getting used to it.

Of course, some demon visitors are more welcome than others. This one was a cute little number. She had close cropped brown hair which framed a round face with big, wide-set almond shaped eyes, a pert little nose, and small, heart-shaped lips. She also had a generous number of curves in all the right places, which the harem outfit she was wearing showed off with distracting clarity. The only trouble was, she was tiny. Not "small," mind you . . . tiny.

The figure in front of me, delectable as it might be, was only about four inches high and floated in midair.

"Hi!" the diminutive lady chirped in a musical voice. "You must be Skeeve. I'm Daphnie."

There was a time when I would have found the effect unsettling.

Courtesy of my recent travels, however, I had seen it before.

"Don't tell me, let me guess," I said in my most off-worldly, casual manner. "You're a Djin. Right? From Djinger?"

"Well . . . a Djeanie, actually. But if we're going to be friends, no wise cracks about the Djeanie with the light brown hair. Okay?"

I stared at her for a moment, waiting her to provide the rest of what was obviously supposed to be a joke. Instead of continuing, though, she simply looked back at me expectantly.

"Okay," I agreed finally. "That shouldn't be hard."

She peered at me for a moment longer, then shook her head.

"You must be the only one in the known dimensions who doesn't know that song," she said. "Are you *sure* you're Skeeve? The Great Skeeve?"

"Well . . . yes. Do we know each other?"

Realizing how stupid the question was, I hastened to modify it before she could answer.

"No. I'm sure I would have remembered if we had met before."

For some reason, my clumsy recovery seemed to please her.

"That's sweet," she said, floating forward to run a soft hand along my cheek, light as a butterfly's touch. "No. I haven't had the pleasure. We have a mutual acquaintance, though. Do you remember a Djin named Kalvin?"

"Kalvin? Sure. He gave me a hand a while back when I was on Perv."

"On Perv, eh?" she said, looking lost in thought for a moment, but then she brightened. "Well he mentioned you and said that if I was ever out this way, I should drop in and say 'Hi' for him."

"Really? That's nice of him . . . I mean, you."

I was pleasantly surprised by Kalvin's thoughtfulness. I don't get many social visitors from off world, mostly just those who are looking for help on one thing or another. It also occurred to me that I had never thought of dropping in to pay social calls to any of the various people I had met on my many adventures,

and made a mental note to correct that situation.

"So, how's Kalvin doing? Is he fitting back into life on Djinger okay after being gone so long?"

"Oh. He's okay," the Djeanie said shrugging her shoulders . . . which had an interesting effect on a shapely body in a harem outfit. "You know how it is. It always takes a while to get back in stride after a sabbatical."

"Say . . . if we're going to be talking for a while, would you mind enlarging to my size? It would make conversation easier."

To be honest with you, after having watched what happened when she shrugged her shoulders, I was interested in seeing her body on a larger scale. If nothing else, it would get rid of the uncomfortable feeling that I was getting physically interested in a talking doll.

"No problem," she said, and waved her arms.

The air rippled and shimmered, and she was standing in front of me at my size. Well, actually, a little less than a head shorter than me, which placed me in the tantalizing position of looking down on her.

"Say, is this a monastery or something?"

"What? Oh. No, this is the Royal Palace of Possiltum." I said. "Why? Do I look like a monk?"

That was, of course, supposed to be a trick question. I was really rather proud of my wardrobe these days, and any monk who dressed the way I did was way out of line with his vows of poverty.

"Not really," she admitted. "But you seem to be showing an awful lot of interest in my cleavage for someone who's supposed to be as well traveled as the Great Skeeve. Don't they have women on this dimensions?"

I guess I had been staring a bit, but hadn't expected her to notice . . . or, if she did, to comment on it. However if there's one thing my years with Aahz have taught me, it's how to cover my shortcomings with words.

"Yes, we have women here," I said with an easy smile. "Frankly, though, I think your cleavage would be stared at no matter what dimension you visited."

She dimpled and preened visibly.

"As starable as it is, however," I continued casually, "my actual interest was professional. Aside from Kalvin, you're the only native of Djinger that I've met, and I was wondering if that stunt you do changing size is a disguise spell, or if it's true shape shifting."

Not bad for a quick out from an embarrassing situation, if I do say so myself. Anyway, Daphnie seemed to accept it.

"Oh that," she said, shrugging her shoulders again. This time, however, I managed to maintain eye contact. No sense pushing my luck. "It's the real thing . . . shape shifting, that is. It's one of the first things a Djin . . . or, especially a Djeanie . . . has to learn. When your whole dimension is the wish biz, you've got to be able to cater to all kinds of fantasies."

My mind went a little out of focus for a moment as it darted across several unprintable fantasies I could think of involving Daphnie, but she was still going.

"It's not just size either . . . well, height, I mean. We can shift to any proportions necessary for the local pin-up standards. Check this out."

With that, she proceeded to treat me to one of the most impressive arrays of female bodies I've ever seen . . . except they were all her! In quick succession, she became willowy, then buxom, then long-legged, while at the same time changing her hair length and color, as well as changing her complexion from delicately pale to a darker hue than her normal cinnamon hue. I decided then and there that where ever this Pinup dimension was, I should make a point of dropping in for a visit . . . soon.

My other reaction was far less predictable. Maybe it was because I had been thinking so much about women and marriage lately, but, while watching her demonstrating her shape shifting skills, it popped into my head that she would be an interesting wife. I mean, think of it: a woman who could assume any size, shape, or personality at will! It would certainly ease the fears of being bored living with one woman for the rest of your life.

"Very impressive," I said, forcing my previous train of thought to a halt. "Tell me, have you ever considered a career in modeling?"

Daphnie's eyes narrowed for a moment, then her face relaxed again.

"I'll assume that was meant as a compliment. Right?" she said.

That one had me really confused.

"Of course," I said. "Why? Isn't it?"

"I'm so attractive, I could make a living at it. Is that what you were thinking?"

"Well . . . Yes. Even though when you put it that way, it *does* sound a little dubious."

"You don't know the half of it," the Djeanie said, rolling her eyes.

"Look, Skeeve. I tried that game once . . . and you're right, I can do it and there's good money in it. It's what goes with it that's a pain."

"I don't understand," I admitted.

"First of all, even though the job may look glamourous from the outside, it isn't. It's long hours in uncomfortable conditions, you know? I mean, it's fun for most people to go to the beach, but try sitting in the same spot for six hours while waves break over you so the jerk photographer can get 'just the right look and lighting' . . . and even then more often than not they don't use the shot."

I nodded sympathetically, all the while wondering what a photographer was and why she would hold still while he shot at her.

"Then again folks think there's a lot of status attached to being a model." she continued. "There's about as much status as being a side of beef on a butcher's block. You may be the center of attention, but to the people working with you, you're just so many pounds of meat to be positioned and marketed. Now mind you, I like having my body touched as much as the next woman, but I like to think that while it's going on, whoever's doing it is thinking of *me*. The way it is, it's like you're a mannequin or a puppet being maneuvered for effect."

"Uh-huh," I said, thinking that if I ever got a chance to touch her body, I'd certainly be keeping my mind on her in the process.

"Of course, there's always the job of keeping the equipment in shape. Most women feel they'd look better if they lost a couple pounds or firmed up the muscle tone . . . and they even work at it occasionally. Well, let me tell you, when your livlihood depends on your looks, keeping the bod in shape is more than a leisure-time hobby. It's a full-time project. Your whole life is centered around diets and exercise, not to mention maintaining your complexion and hair. Sure, I have an advantage because I can shape shift, but believe me, the less you have to do magikally, the less strain you put on the system and the longer the machine lasts."

"Which brings up another point: Whatever you do to maintain your looks, it's a losing fight with time. Djeanies may have a longer life span than some of the women from other dimensions, but eventually age catches up with everyone. Strategic features that once used to catch the eye start to droop and sag, the skin on the neck and hands starts to look more and more like wet tissue paper, and faster than you can say 'old crone,' you're back out the door and they've replaced you from the bottomless pool of young hopefuls. Terrific, huh?"

That one made me think a bit. One thing about being a magician was that age wasn't a prime factor. Heck, for a while when I was starting out, I used my disguise spell to make myself look older because no one would believe that a young magician would be any good. The idea of losing one's job simply because one had grown older was a terrifying concept. I found myself being glad that most jobs didn't have the age restrictions that modeling seemed to.

"Then, just to top things off," the Djeanie said, "there's the minor detail of how people treat you. Most men are intimidated by your looks and won't come near you on a bet. They'll stare and drool, and maybe fantasize a little, but they won't try to date you. Unless they have stellar looks themselves or an iron-clad ego, they're afraid of creating a 'Beauty and the Beast' comparison. The ones who do come on to you usually have a specific scenario in mind . . . and that doesn't involve you either talking or thinking at all. They want an ornament, and if there's actually a person inside that glamourous package, they're not only surprised, they're a little annoyed."

She sighed and shook her head.

"Sorry to ramble like that, but it's a pet peeve of mine. When you stop to think about it, it's a little sad to think of women who feel that all they have to offer the world is their looks. Personally, I like to think I have more to offer than that."

Taking a deep breath, she blew it all out noisily, then smiled and cocked her head at me.

"Um . . . How about if I just say that I think you look fantastic, and forget about speculating on your potential as a model?" I said cautiously.

"Then I'd say 'Thank you kind sir'. You aren't so bad looking yourself."

She smiled and made a small curtsey. I successfully resisted an impulse to bow back to her.

Mostly, I was trying to think of what we could talk about next, having exhausted the subject of beauty.

"So, how do you know Kalvin?" Daphnie said, solving the problem for me. "He made it sound like the two of you were old buddies."

Now we were back on familiar footing.

"Actually, I bought him over at the Bazaar at Deva. Well, to be accurate, I bought his bottle. I only was entitled to one wish from him . . . but I don't need to explain that to you. You probably know the drill better than I do. I didn't get to know him until a couple years later when I got around to opening the bottle."

"I don't understand," she said, frowning prettily. "Why did you buy his bottle if you weren't going to use it for several years?"

"Why I bought it in the first place is a long story," I said, rolling my eyes comically. "As to why I didn't use it for so long, I'm part of a fairly impressive team of magik users . . . the head of it, actually. We do a pretty good job of handling most problems that come up on our own without calling on outside help."

Okay. So I was blowing my own trumpet a bit. Even though I didn't know if anything would ever develop between us, she was cute enough that I figured that it couldn't hurt to impress her a little.

"So he was with you the whole time? From when you purchased his bottle until his discharged his duty on Perv? When was that, exactly?"

She didn't seem very impressed. If anything, it was as if she was more interested in asking questions about Kalvin than in learning about me, a situation I found slightly annoying.

"Oh, it wasn't all that long ago," I said. "Just a couple weeks back, in fact. Of course, time doesn't advance at the same rate on all the dimensions . . . as I'm sure you know."

"True," she said, thoughtfully. "Tell me, did he say he was going straight back to Djinger? Or was he going to stop somewhere along the way, first?"

"Let me think. As I recall, he didn't . . . Wait a minute. Didn't he make it back to Djinger? I thought you said that he was the one who told you to look me up."

I was both concerned and confused. If Daphnie was looking for Kalvin, then how had she found out about me? I didn't know any other Djins . . . or anyone who traveled to Djinger on a regular basis.

"Oh, he made it back all right," she shrugged. "I was just a little curious about . . . "

There was a soft BAMF, and a second Djin materialized in the room. This one I recognized immediately as Kalvin, who I had just been speaking to Daphnie about. I could tell at a glance, though, that something was wrong.

Chapter Fifteen

"Blessed are the peacemakers,
for they shall take flack from both sides."
unofficial UN motto

I had gotten to know Kalvin pretty well during my trip to Perv, and all through that adventure he had been as unshakable in a crisis as anyone I had ever known. Now, however, he was exhibiting all the classic symptoms of someone who was about to lose control of his temper . . . clenched teeth, furrowed brow, tight expression, the works.

Fortunately, his anger seemed to be directed at my guest rather than at me.

"I should have known!" he snarled, without so much as a nod to acknowledge my presence. "I should have checked here first as soon as I found out you were gone."

It occurred to me that, as little as I knew about Djins, that it could be markedly unhealthy to have one upset with you. Realizing that magik, like a knife, could be used both benevolently *or* destructively, my first instinct probably would have been to try to calm him down quickly . . . or to vacate the premises.

To my surprise, however, the Djeanie spun around and leveled what seemed to be an equal amount of anger back at him.

"Oh, I see," she spat back. "It's all right for *you* to disappear for years at a time, but as soon as I step out the door, you've got to come looking for me!"

The interest I had been feeling in Daphnie came to a screeching halt. In the space of a few seconds her personality had changed from a flirtatious coquette to a shrill shrew. Then, too, there seemed to be more to her relationship with Kalvin than the "acquaintance" she had billed it as.

"That was business," the Djin was saying, still nose to nose with my visitor. "You know, the stuff that puts food on the table for our whole dimension? Besides, if you were just going out to kick up your heels a bit I wouldn't care. What I DO mind is your sneaking off to check up on me."

"So what? It shouldn't bother you . . . unless you haven't been telling me *everything*, that is."

"What bothers me is that you can't bring yourself to believe me," Kalvin shot back. "Why do you even bother asking me anything if you aren't going to believe I'm telling you the truth?"

"I *used* to believe everything you told me. YOU taught me how stupid that was. Remember?"

This seemed to be going nowhere fast, so I summoned my courage and stepped forward to intervene.

"Excuse me, but I thought you two were friends."

Kalvin broke off his arguing to spare me a withering look.

"Friends? Is that what she told you?"

He rounded on the Djeanie again.

"You know, babe, for someone who keeps accusing me of lying, you play pretty fast and loose with the truth yourself!"

"Don't be silly," the Djeanie said. "If I had told him I was your wife, he would have just covered for you. You think I don't know how you men lie to protect each other?"

"Wait a minute," I interrupted. "Did you say 'wife'? Are you two married?"

Whatever was left of my interest in Daphnie died without a whimper.

"Sure," Kalvin said with a grimace. "Can't you tell by the loving and affection we shower on each other? Of course we're married. Do you think either of us would put up with this abuse from a stranger?"

He gave a brief shake of his head, and for a moment seemed to almost return to normal.

"By the way, Skeeve, good to see you again," he said, flashing a tight smile. "Sorry to have forgotten my manners, but I get . . . Anyway, even though it may be a bit late, I'd like to introduce you to my wife, Daphnie."

"Well, at least now I know what it takes to be introduced to one of your business friends."

And they were off again.

There was a knock on the door.

I answered it, thinking as I did that it was nice to know at least a few people who came into my room the normal way . . . which is to say, by the door . . . instead of simply popping in announced

"Is everything okay, Boss? I thought I heard voices."

"Sure," I said, "it's just . . . Guido?"

My mind had to grapple with several images and concepts simultaneously, and it wasn't doing so hot. First was the realization that Guido was back from his mission as a special tax envoy. Second, that he had his arm in a sling.

The latter probably surprised me more than the former. After all our time together, I had begun to believe that my bodyguards were all but invulnerable. It was a little unsettling to be reminded that they could be hurt physically like anyone else.

"What are you doing back?" I said. "And what happened to your arm?"

Instead of answering, he peered suspiciously past me at the arguing Djins.

"What's goin' on in there, Boss?" he demanded. "Who are those two jokers, anyway?"

I was a little surprised that he could hear and see my visitors, but then I remembered that it's only while a Djin is under contract that he or she can only be seen and heard by the holder of their bottle.

"Oh, those are just a couple friends of mine," I said. "Well . . . sort of friends. I thought they were dropping by to say 'Hi,' but, as you can see, things seem to have gotten a little out of hand. The one with the beard is Kalvin, and the lady he's arguing with is his wife, Daphnie."

I thought it was a fairly straightforward explanation, but Guido recoiled as if I had struck him.

"Did you say 'his wife'?"

"That's right. Why?"

My bodyguard stepped forward to place himself between me and the arguing couple.

"Get out of here, Boss," he said quietly.

"What?"

At first I thought I had misunderstood him.

"Boss," he hissed with aggravated patience. "I'm your body-guard. Right? Well, as your bodyguard and the one currently responsible for the well bein' of your continued health, I'm tellin' you to get out of here!"

"But . . . "

Apparently Guido wasn't willing to debate the point further. Instead, he scooped me up with his good arm and carried me out the door into the corridor, where he deposited me none too gently against the wall beside the doorway.

"Now stay here," he said, shaking a massive finger in my face. "Got that? *Stay here!*"

I recognized the tone of his voice. It was the same as when I tried to give Gleep a simple command . . . for the third or fourth time after he had been steadfastly ignoring me. I decided I would try to prove that I was smarter than my pet by actually following orders.

"Okay, Guido," I said, with a curt nod. "Here it is."

He hesitated for a moment, eyeing me as if to see if I was

going to make a break for the door. Then he gave a little nod of satisfaction, turned, and strode into my room, closing the door behind him.

While I couldn't make out the exact words, I heard the arguing voices cease for a moment. Then they were raised again in angry chorus, punctuated by Guido's voice saying something. Then there was silence.

After a few long moments of stillness, the door opened again.

"You can come in now, Boss," my bodyguard announced. "They're gone."

I left my post by the wall and re-entered my room. A quick glance around was all it took to confirm my bodyguard's claim. The Djins had departed for destinations unknown. Surprisingly enough, my immediate reaction was to be a little hurt that they hadn't bothered to say goodbye.

I also realized that I wanted a goblet of wine, but suppressed the desire. Instead, I perched on the side of the bed.

"All right, Guido," I said. "What was all that about?"

"Sorry to barge in like that, Boss," my bodyguard said, not looking at all apologetic. "You know that's not my normal style."

"So what were you doing?"

"What I was doin' was my job," he retorted. "As your bodyguard, I was attemptin' to protect you from bein' hurt or maybe even killed. It's what you pay me for, accordin' my job description."

"Protecting me? From those two? Com'on, Guido. They were just arguing. They weren't even arguing with me. It was a family squabble between the two of them."

"*Just arguing?*" my bodyguard said, looming over me. "*What do you think . . .* "

He broke off suddenly and stepped back, breathing heavy.

I was genuinely puzzled. I couldn't recall having seen Guido more upset, but I really couldn't figure out what was bothering him.

"Sorry, Boss," he said finally, in a more normal tone. "I'm still a little worked up after that close call. I'll be all right in a second."

"What close call?" I pressed. "They were just . . . "

"I know, I know," he said, waving me to silence. "they were just arguing."

He took a deep breath and flexed his arms and hands.

"You know, Boss, I keep forgettin' how inexperienced you are. I mean, you may be tops in the magik department, but when it comes to my specialty, which is to say rough and tumble stuff, you're still a babe in the woodwork."

A part of me wanted to argue this, since I had been in some pretty nasty scrapes over the years, but I kept my mouth shut. Guido and his cousin Nunzio were specialists, and if nothing else over the years I've learned to respect expertise.

"You see, Boss, people say that guys like me and Nunzio are not really all that different from the cops . . . that it's the same game on different sides of the line. I dunno. It may be true. What I am sure of, though, is that both we and our counterparts agree on one thing: The most dangerous situation to stick your head into . . . the situation most likely to get you dead fast . . . isn't a shoot out or a gang war. It's an ordinary D&D scenario."

"D&D," I frowned. "You mean that game you were telling me about with the maps and the dice?"

"No. I'm talkin' about a 'domestic disturbance.' A family squabble . . . just like you had goin' on here when I came in. They're deadly, Boss. Especially ones between a husband and wife."

I wanted to laugh, but he seemed to be utterly serious about what he was saying.

"Are you kidding, Guido?" I said. "What could happen that would be dangerous?"

"More things that you can imagine," he replied. "That's what makes them so dangerous. In regular hassles, you can pretty much track what's going on and what might happen next. Arguments between a husband and wife are unpredictable, though. You can't tell who's gonna swing at who, when or with what, because they don't know themselves."

I was beginning to believe what he was saying. The concept was both fascinating and frightening.

"Why do you think that is, Guido? What makes fights between married couples so explosive?"

My bodyguard frowned and scratched his head.

"I never really gave it much thought," he said. "If I had to give an opinion, I'd say it was due to the motivationals."

"The motives?" I corrected without thinking.

"That too," he nodded. "You see, Boss, the business-type disputes which result in violence like I am normally called upon to deal with have origins that are easily comprehended . . . . like greed or fear. That is to say, either Boss A wants somethin' that Boss B is reluctant to part with, as in a good sized hunk of revenue generatin' territory, or Boss B is afraid that Boss A is gonna try to whack him and decides to beat him to the punch. In these situationals, there is a clear cut objective in mind, and the action is therefore relatively easy to predict and counter. Know what I mean?"

"I think so," I said. "And in a domestic disturbance?"

"That's where it can get ugly," he grimaced. "It starts out with people arguin' when they don't know why they're arguin.' What's at stake there is emotions and hurt feelin's, not money. The problem with that is that there is no clear cut objective, and as a result, there is no way of tellin' when the fightin' should cease. It just keeps escalatin' up and up, with both sides dishin' out and takin' more and more damage, until each of 'em is hurt so bad that the only important thing left is to hurt the other one back."

He smacked his fist loudly into his other hand, wincing slightly when he moved his injured arm.

"When it explodes," he continued, "you don't want to be anywhere near ground zero. One will go at the other, or they'll go at each other, with anything that's at hand. The worst part is, and the reason neither us or the cops want to try to mess with it, is that if you try to break it up, chances are that they'll both turn on you. You see, mad as they are, they'll still reflexively protect each other from any outside force . . . into which category will fall you or anyone else who tries to interfere.

That's why the best policy, if you have a choice at all, is to get away from them and wait until the dust settles before venturin' close again."

This was all very interesting, particularly since I was in the middle of contemplating marriage myself. However my bodyguard's wince had reminded me of the unanswered questions originally raised by his appearance.

"I think I understand now, Guido," I said. "Thanks. Now tell me, what happened to your arm? And what are you doing back at the palace?"

Guido seemed a little taken aback at the sudden change of topic.

"Sorry I didn't check in as soon as I got back, Boss," he said, looking uncomfortable. "It was late and I thought you were already asleep . . . until I heard that argument in process, that is. I would have let you know first thing in the morning."

"Uh huh," I said. "No problem. But since we're talking now, what happened?"

"We ran into a little trouble, is all," he said, looking away. "Nothin' serious."

"Serious enough to put your arm in a sling," I observed. "So what happened?"

"If it's okay with you, Boss, I'd rather not go into details. Truth is, it's more than a little embarrassing."

I was about to insist, then thought better of it. Guido never asked for much from me, but it seemed right now he was asking that I not push the point. The least I could do was respect his privacy.

"All right," I said slowly. "We'll let it ride for now. Will you be able to work with that arm?"

"In a pinch, maybe. But not at peak efficiency," he admitted. "That's really what I wanted to talk to you about, Boss. Is there any chance you can assign Nunzio to be Pookie's backup while I take over his duties here?"

Realizing how infatuated Guido was with Pookie, it was quite a request. Still, I was reluctant to go along with it.

"I don't know, Guido," I said. "Nunzio's been working with Gleep to try to figure out what's wrong with him. I kind of hate to pull him off that until we have some answers. Tell you what. How about if I talk to Chumley about helping out?"

"Chumley?" my bodyguard frowned. "I dunno, Boss. Don't you think that him bein' a troll would tend to scare folks in these parts?"

Realizing that both Guido and Nunzio relied heavily on intimidation in their work, this was an interesting objection. Still, he had a point.

"Doesn't Pookie have a disguise spell or something that could soften Chumley's appearance?" I suggested. "I was assuming that she wasn't wandering around the countryside showing the green scales of a Pervect."

"Hey! That's right! Good idea, Boss," Guido said, brightening noticeably. "In that case, no problem. Chumley's as stand up as they come."

"Okay, I'll talk to him first thing in the morning."

"Actually, Chumley's a better choice that Nunzio," my bodyguard continued, almost to himself. "Pookie's still kinda upset over shootin' me, and Nunzio would probably . . . "

"Whoa! Wait a minute! Did you say that *Pookie* shot you?"

Guido looked startled for a moment, then he drew himself up into a wall of righteous indignation.

"Really, Boss," he said. "I thought we agreed that we wasn't gonna talk about this. Not for a while, anyway."

Chapter Sixteen

*"Marriage is a fine institution . . .
if one requires institutionalizing."*
S. Freud

"Hi, Chumley. Mind if I come in?"

The troll looked up from his book, and his enormous mouth twisted into a grin of pleasure.

"Skeeve, old boy!" he said. "Certainly. As a matter of fact, I've been expecting you."

"Really?" I said, stepping into his room and looking around for somewhere to sit.

"Yes. I ran into Guido this morning, and he explained the situation to me. He said you were going to be calling on me for a bit of work. I was just killing time waiting for the official word, is all."

I wondered if the briefing my bodyguard had given Chumley was any more detailed than what he and told me.

"It's all right with you, then?" I said. "You don't mind?"

"Tish tosh. Think nothing of it," the troll said. "Truth to tell, I'll be glad to have a specific assignment again. I've been feeling a bit at loose ends lately. In fact, I was starting to wonder why I was staying around at all."

That touched a nerve in me. It had been some time since I had even stopped by to say 'Hello' to Chumley.

"Sorry if I've been a bit distant," I said guiltily. "I've been . . . busy . . . and . . . "

"Quite right," Chumley said with a grin and a wink. "Caught a glimpse of your workload when you rolled in the other night. Bit of all right, that."

I think I actually blushed.

"No really," I stammered. "I've been . . . "

"Relax, old boy," the troll waved. "I was just pulling your leg a bit. I know you've been up against it, what with the Queen after you and all. By the by, I've got a few thoughts on that, but I figured it would be rude to offer advice when none had been asked for."

"You do? That's terrific," I said, and meant it. "I've been meaning to ask your opinion, but wasn't sure how to bring it up."

"I believe you just have, actually," Chumley grinned. "Pull up a chair."

I followed his instructions as he continued.

"Advice on marriage, particularly when it comes to the selection of the partner to be, is usually best kept to oneself. The recipients usually already have their minds made up, and voicing any opinion contradictory to their decision can be hazardous to one's health. Since you've actually gotten around to asking, however, I think you might find my thoughts on the matter to be a tad surprising."

"How's that?"

"Well, most blokes who know me . . . the real me, that is, rather than Big Crunch . . . think of me as a bit of a romantic."

I blinked, but kept a straight face.

While I have the utmost respect for Chumley, I had never thought of him as a romantic figure . . . possibly something to do with his green matted hair and huge eyes of different sizes. While I supposed that trolls have love lives (otherwise, how does one get little trolls?) I'd have to rate their attractiveness in

relation to dwellers of other dimensions to be way down near the bottom. Their female counterparts, the trollops such as his sister Tananda, were a whole different story, of course, but for the trolls themselves . . . on a scale of one to ten, I'd generously score them around negative eighteen.

This particular troll, however, old friend though he might be, was currently sitting within an arm's length of me . . . his arm, not mine . . . and as that arm was substantially stronger than two arms of the strongest human . . . which I'm not . . . I decided not to argue the point with him. Heck, if he wanted to say he was the Queen of May I'd probably agree with him.

"For the most part, they'd be right," Chumley was continuing, "but on the subject of marriage, I can be as coldly analytical as the best of them."

"Terrific," I said. "That's what I was really hoping for . . . . an unemotional, unbiased opinion."

"First, let me ask you a few questions," the troll said.

"All right."

"Do you love her?"

I paused to give the question an honest consideration.

"I don't think so," I said. "Of course, I really don't know all that much about love."

"Does she love you?"

"Again, I don't think so," I said.

I was actually enjoying this. Chumley was breaking things down to where even I could understand his logic.

"Well, has she said she loves you?"

That one I didn't even have to think about.

"No."

"You're sure?" the troll pressed.

"Positive," I said. "The closest she's come is to say she thinks we'd make a good pair. I *think* she meant it as a compliment."

"Good," my friend said, settling back in his chair.

"Excuse me?" I blinked. "For a moment there, I thought you said . . . "

"I said 'Good', and I meant it," the troll repeated.

"You lost me there," I said. "I thought marriages were supposed to be . . . "

" . . . Based on love?" Chumley finished for me. "That's what most young people think. That's also why so many of their marriages fall apart."

Even though he had sort of warned me in advance, I found the troll's position to be a bit unsettling.

"Um, Chumley? Are we differentiating between 'analytical' and 'cynical'?"

"It's not really as insensitive as it sounds, Skeeve," the troll said with a laugh, apparently unoffended by my comment. "You see, when you're young and full of hormones, and come in close contact for the first time with someone of the opposite sex who isn't related to you, you experience feelings and urges that you've never encountered before. Now since, despite their bragging to the contrary, most people are raised to think of themselves as good and decent folks, they automatically attach the socially correct label to these feelings: Love. Of course, there's also a socially correct response when two people feel that way about each other . . . specifically, marriage."

"But isn't that . . . " I began, but the troll held up a restraining hand.

"Hear me out," he said. "Now, continuing with our little saga, eventually passions cool, and the infatuation has run it's course. It might take years, but eventually they find that 'just being together' isn't enough. It's time to get on with life. Unfortunately, right about then they discover that they have little if anything in common. All too often they find that their goals in life are different, or, at the very least, their plans on how to achieve them don't coincide. Then they find, instead of the ideal partner to stand back to back with while taking on the world, they've actually opened a second front. That is, they have to spend as much or more time dealing with each other as they do the rest of the world."

Despite myself, I found I was being drawn in, almost mesmerized, by his oration.

"What happens then?" I said.

"If they are at all rational . . . notice I said 'rational,' not 'intelligent' . . . they go their separate ways. All too often, however, they cling to the concept of 'love' and try to 'make it work.' When that happens, the result is an armed camp living an uneasy truce . . . and nobody's happy . . . or actually achieving their full potential."

I thought about the bickering I had recently witnessed between Kalvin and Daphnie, and about what Guido had told me about domestic disturbances and how they can explode into violence. In spite of myself, I shuddered involuntarily.

"That sounds grim," I said.

"Oh, it is," the troll nodded. "Trying to 'make it work' is the most frustrating, depressing pastime ever invented. The real problem is that they've each ended up with the wrong person, but rather than admit that, they try to gloss things over with cosmetics."

"Cosmetics?"

"Surface changes. Things that really don't matter."

"I don't get it."

"All right," the troll said. "I'll give you an example. The wife says she needs some new clothes, so her husband gives her some money to go out shopping. That's a rather simple and straight forward exchange, wouldn't you say?"

"Well . . . yes."

"Only on the surface," Chumley explained. "Now look at it a little deeper . . . at what's *really* going on. The husband has been getting caught up in his work . . . that's a normal reaction for a man when he get's married and starts feeling 'responsible,' by the way . . . and his wife is feeling unhappy and ignored. Her solution is that she needs some new clothes to make her more attractive so her husband will pay more attention to her. A surface solution to her unhappiness. Now, when she says she needs new clothes, the husband is annoyed because she seems to have a closet full of clothes that she never wears, but rather than argue with her, he gives her some money for shopping . . .

again, a surface solution. You'll notice that he simply gives her the money. He doesn't *take* her shopping and help her find some new outfits."

The troll leaned back in his chair and folded his arms.

"From there, it goes downhill. She gets some new clothes and wears them, but the husband either doesn't notice or doesn't comment . . . possibly because he still resents having to pay for what he thinks is a needless purchase. Therefore, buying new clothes . . . her surface solution . . . doesn't work because she still feels ignored and unhappy . . . and a little angry and frustrated that her husband doesn't seem to appreciate her no matter how hard she tries. Her husband, in the meantime, senses that she's still unhappy so that giving her money . . . *his* surface solution . . . didn't work. He feels even more bitter and resentful because now it seems that his wife is going to be upset and unhappy even if he 'gives her everything she's asked for'. You see, by trying to deal with the problem with surface, cosmetic gestures without acknowledging to themselves the real issues, they've actually made things worse instead of better."

He smiled triumphantly as I considered his thesis.

"So you're saying that marriages don't work," I said carefully. "that the concept itself if flawed."

"Not at all," the troll corrected, shaking his head. "I was saying that getting married under the mistaken impression that love conquers all is courting disaster. A proper match between two people who enter into a marriage with their eyes open and free of romantic delusions can result in a much happier life together than they could ever have alone."

"All right," I said. "If love and romance are bad bases for deciding to marry someone because it's too easy to fool yourself, what would you see as a *valid* reason to get married."

"There are lots of them," Chumley shrugged. "Remember when Hemlock first arrived here? Her marriage to Roderick was a treaty and a merger between two kingdoms. It's common among royalty, but you'll find similar matches in the business world as well. In that case, both sides knew what they wanted and could expect, so it worked out fine."

"Sorry, but that seems a bit cold to me," I said, shaking my head.

"Really?" the troll cocked his head. "Maybe I'm phrasing this wrong. What you *don't* want is a situation where there is a hidden agenda on either or both sides. Everything should be up front and on the table . . . like with the Hemlock/Roderick marriage."

"What's a hidden agenda?"

"Hmmm . . . That one's a little hard to explain. Tell me, if you married Queen Hemlock, what would you expect?"

That one caught me totally unprepared.

"I don't know . . . nothing, really," I managed, at last. "I guess I figure that it would pretty much be a marriage in name only, with her going her way and me going mine."

"Good," the troll said emphatically.

"Good?" I echoed. "Com'on, Chumley."

"Good in that you aren't expecting anything. You aren't going into it with the notion of reforming her, or that she'd give up her throne to hover around you adoringly, or any one of a myriad of other false hopes or assumptions that most grooms have on the way to the altar."

"I suppose that's good," I said.

"Good? It's vital," the troll insisted. "Too many people marry the person they *think* their partner will become. They have some sort of idea that a marriage ceremony is somehow magical. That it will eliminate all the dubious traits and habits their partner had when they were single. That's about as unrealistic as if you had expected Aahz to stop being a money-grubber or to shed his temper just because you signed on as an apprentice. Anyway, when their partner keeps right on being the person he or she has been all along, they feel hurt and betrayed. Since they believe that there *should* have been a change, the only conclusion they can reach is that their love wasn't enough to trigger it . . . or, more likely, that there's something wrong with their partner. *That's* when marriages start getting bloody.

At least with Queen Hemlock's proposal, nobody's kidding anybody about what's going to happen."

I mulled over his words for a few moments.

"So you're saying that you think I should marry Queen Hemlock," I said.

"Here now. Hold on," the troll said, leaning back and holding up his hands. "I said no such thing. That's the kind of decision that only you can make. I was just commenting on what I see as the more common pitfalls of marriage, is all. If you *do* decide to marry the Queen, there are certain aspects that would weigh in favor of it working . . . but you're the one who has to decide what you want out of a marriage and whether or not this is it."

Terrific. I had been hoping that Chumley's analytic approach would simplify things for me. Instead, he had simply added a wagon load of other factors to be considered. I needed that like Deva needed more merchants.

"Well, I appreciate the input, Chumley," I said, rising from my seat. "You've given me a lot to think about."

"Think nothing of it, old boy. Glad to help."

"And you're all set with the assignment? Guido told you how to hook up with Pookie?"

"Right-o."

I started to go, but paused for one more question.

"By the way, Chumley. Have you ever been married yourself?"

"Me?" the troll seemed genuinely surprised. "Gracious no. Why do you ask?"

"Just curious," I said, and headed out the door.

Chapter Seventeen

"What am I supposed to do with all this gold?"
Midas, Rex

At this point, I had to admit that I was more confused than ever. It seemed that everyone I talked to had a different view of marriage, which wasn't making my decision any easier. One thing everyone seemed to agree on, though: A bad marriage could be a living Hell.

Of course, defining what a good marriage was and how to avoid a bad one seemed to defy simple explanation . . . or, at least, one simple enough that I could grasp.

The problem was, as limited as my experience with the opposite sex was, my knowledge of marriages, good or bad, was even sketchier. I could barely remember my own family, I had left home so long ago. The only married couple I had met on my adventures was the Woof Writers, and realizing they were werewolves I somehow didn't think that they were a valid role model for me. Then again, Massha and Badaxe were talking about getting married. Maybe they could provide some insight for me.

I was considering this possibility as I wandered across the

palace courtyard, when a voice interrupted my thoughts.

"Hey, Partner!"

I had to look around for a moment before I spotted Aahz waving at me from one of the palace's upper windows.

"Where were you this morning? We missed you at the session with Grimble."

"I had to talk to Chumley," I called back. "Guido got hurt, and I had to ask Chumley to stand in for him."

"Whatever," my partner waved. "Go see Grimble. It's important!"

That sounded vaguely ominous, but Aahz seemed chipper enough.

"What's up?"

"Day of the eagle," he yelled, and disappeared from sight.

Terrific!

As I redirected my steps toward Grimble's office, I couldn't help but feel a little annoyed. I mean, with all the other problems plaguing me, I really didn't need the added distraction of talking to Grimble about some bird sanctuary.

"Hi, Grimble. Aahz said you wanted to see me?"

The Chancellor glanced up to where I was leaning against the doorway.

"Ah. Lord Skeeve," he nodded. "Yes. Come in. This shouldn't take long."

I eased into the room and plopped down in the offered chair.

"What's the problem? Aahz said something about eagles?"

"Eagles? I wonder what he was referring to. No, there's no problem," Grimble said. "If anything, quite the contrary. In fact, the new tax collection process is working well enough that we're now in a positive cash flow situation. What's more, I think that except for dotting a few I's and crossing a few T's we've got the new budget pretty well nailed down."

He leaned back and favored me with one of his rare smiles.

"Speaking of 'tease,' that's quite a little assistant you have there. I'll admit I'm very impressed with *all* her qualifications. Take my advice and don't let her go . . . as if I had to tell you that."

This was, of course, accompanied by a smirk and a wink.

While I had grown to expect this sort of comment from Grimble whenever the subject of Bunny came up, I found I was no more fond of it than when they had first met. At least now, he was refraining from such behavior in her presence . . . which was a victory of sorts, I suppose. Still, I was annoyed and decided to take another shot at it.

"I'm surprised to hear you talk that way, Grimble," I said. "Are you really so hung up on hormones that you can't just acknowledge her worth as a colleague *without* adding sexual innuendos?"

"Well . . . I . . . " the Chancellor began, but I cut him off.

" . . . Especially realizing that the Queen . . . you know, your employer? . . . is also female. I wonder if she's aware of your slanted views regarding her gender, or, if she isn't, how she'd react if she found out. Do you think she'd just fire you, or would she want to see if you were bluffing, first. From what I can tell, she's as interested in playing around as you claim to be."

Grimble actually blanched, which realizing how pale his complexion was to start with, was quite a sight.

"You wouldn't tell her, Would you, Lord Skeeve?" he stammered. "I meant no disrespect to Bunny. Really. She has one of the best financial minds it's been my privilege to work with . . . male or female. I was just trying to make a little joke. You know, man to man? It's one of the rituals of male bonding."

"Not with all males," I pointed out. "Relax, though. You should know me well enough by now to realize it's not my style to go running to the Queen with reports or complaints. Just don't push it so hard in the future. Okay?"

"Thank you, Lord Skeeve. I . . . Thanks. I'll make a point of it."

"Now then," I said, starting to rise, "I assume that we're done here? That the report on the collections and budget was what you wanted to see me about?"

"No, that was just a casual update," Grimble corrected,

back on familiar ground now. "The real reason I had to see you was this."

He reached somewhere on the floor behind him and produced a large bag which jingled as he plopped it onto his desk.

"I don't understand," I said, eying the bag. "What is it?"

"It's your wages," he smiled. "I know that normally you let your assistants handle these matters, but realizing the amount involved due to your promotion, I thought you might like to deal with it personally."

I stared at the bag uncomfortably. It was a very big bag.

Even though I had been persuaded by Aahz and Bunny to accept a sizable wage for my services, looking at a number on a piece of paper was a lot different that actually seeing the equivalent in hard cash.

Perhaps it wouldn't seem like so much after I had paid the others their share . . .

"Your assistants have already picked up their wages," Grimble was saying, "so this is the last payment to complete this round of payroll. If you'll just sign here?"

He pushed a slip of paper across the desk at me, but I ignored it and kept staring at the money bag.

It was a *very* large bag. Especially considering how little I was actually doing.

"Is something wrong, Lord Skeeve?"

For a moment, I actually considered telling him what was bothering me, which is a sign of how upset I was. Grimble is not someone you confide in.

"No. Nothing," I said instead.

"Would you like to count it?" he pressed, apparently still unconvinced.

"Why? Didn't you?"

"Of course I did," the Chancellor bristled, his professional pride stung. I forced a smile.

"Good enough for me. Checking your work would be a waste of both our time, don't you agree?"

I quickly scribbled my name on the receipt, gathered up the

bag, and left, carefully ignoring the puzzled look Grimble was leveling at me.

"You gonna need us for anything, Boss? You want we should hang around out here?"

"Whatever, Guido," I waved absently as I shut the door. "I'm going to be here for a while, though, if you want to get something to eat. I've got a lot to think over."

"Oh, we already ate. So we'll just . . . "

The door closed and cut off the rest of whatever it was he was saying.

Guido and Nunzio had materialized at my side somewhere during my walk back from Grimble's. I wasn't sure exactly when, as I had been lost in thought and they hadn't said anything until we reached my room. If I had realized they were there, I probably would have had one of them carry the bag of gold for me. It was heavy. Very heavy.

Setting the burden down on my desk, I sank into a chair and stared at it. I had heard of bad pennies coming back to haunt someone, but this was ridiculous.

I had been so absorbed in trying to make up my mind about Queen Hemlock that I hadn't gotten around to my self-appointed task of trying to cut back on my staff or otherwise reduce the M.Y.T.H. Inc. bill to the kingdom. Now, I had the money in hand, and all I felt was guilty.

No matter what Aahz and Bunny said, it still felt wrong to me. Here we were, cutting corners on the budget and squeezing taxes out of the populace to try to shore up the kingdom's financial woes, while I siphoned money out of the treasury that I didn't really need. What was more, since it was my procrastinating on staff cuts that had resulted in the inflated payday, I certainly didn't think I should be rewarded for it.

The more I thought about it, the more determined I became to figure out some way to give the money back. Of course, it would have to be done quietly, almost secretly, or I'd suffer the wrath of both Aahz and Bunny. Still, to me it was necessary if I was going to be able to live with myself.

Then, too, there was the problem of how to reduce our payroll. Actually, if what Grimble had just told me was accurate, that situation might take care of itself. If the budget was coming into balance, and if the collection process was now flowing smoothly, then I could probably send Bunny aback to Deva, as well as one or more of my bodyguards. What was more, I could then insist on removing my own payment as financial counselor. All that should reduce the M.Y.T.H. Inc. bill substantially.

That still left me with the problem of how to deal with the disproportionate payment I had already received.

Then an idea struck me. I'd do what any other executive would do when confronted with a problem: I'd delegate it to someone else!

Striding to the door, I opened it and looked into the hall. Sure enough, my two bodyguards were still there, apparently embroiled in conversation with each other.

"Guido! Nunzio!" I called. "Come in here for a second."

I re-entered the room and returned to my desk without waiting to see if they were responding. I needn't have worried.

By the time I had re-seated myself, they were standing in front of me.

"I have a little assignment for you boys," I said, smiling.

"Sure, Boss," they chimed in chorus.

"But first, I want to check something. As long as I've known you, you've both made it clear that, it the past, you've had no qualms about bending the rules as situations called for it, working outside the law as it were. Is that correct?"

"That's right."

"No problem."

I noticed that, though to the affirmative, their answers were slower and less enthusiastic than before.

"All right. The job I have for you has to be done secretly, with nobody knowing that I'm behind it. Not even Aahz or Bunny. Understand?"

My bodyguards looked even more uncomfortable that before, but nodded their agreement.

"Okay, Here's the job," I said, pushing the bag of money towards them. "I want you to take this money and get rid of it."

The two men stared at me, then exchanged glances.

"I don't quite get you, Boss," Guido said at last. "What do you want us to do with it?"

"I don't care and I don't want to know," I said. "I just want this money back in circulation within the kingdom. Spend it or give it to charity."

Just then an idea hit me.

"Better still, figure out some way of passing it around to those people who have been complaining that they can't pay their taxes."

Guido frowned and glanced at his cousin again.

"I dunno, Boss," he said carefully. "It don't seem right, somehow. I mean, we're supposed to be collectin' taxes from people . . . not givin' it to them."

"What Guido means," Nunzio put in, "is that our speciality is extracting funds from people and institutions. Givin' it back is a little out of our line."

"Well then I guess it's about time you expanded your horizons," I said, unmoving. "Anyway, that's the assignment. Understand?"

"Yes, Boss," they chorused, still looking uneasy.

"And remember, not a word about this to the rest of the team."

"If you say so, Boss."

As I've said, the bag was heavy enough to have given me trouble carrying it, but Guido gathered it up easily with his one good hand, then stood hefting it for a moment.

"Umm . . . Are you *sure* you want to do this, Boss?" he said. "It don't seem right, somehow. Most folks would have to work for a lifetime to earn this much money."

"That's my point," I muttered.

"Huh?"

"Never mind," I said. "I'm sure. Now do it. Okay?"

155

"Consider it done."

They didn't quite salute, but they drew themselves up and nodded before they headed for the door. I recalled they had been working with the army for a while, and guessed that it had rubbed off on them more than they realized.

After they had gone, I leaned back and savored the moment.

I actually felt *good!* It seemed that I had found a solution to at least one of my problems.

Maybe that had been my difficulty all this time. I had been trying to focus on too many unrelated problems at once. Now that the whole money thing was off my back, I could devote my entire attention to the Queen Hemlock situation without interruptions or distractions.

For the first time in a long while, I actually felt optimistic about being able to arrive at a decision.

Chapter Eighteen

"It's so easy, a child could do it!"
The legal disclaimer found on the instruction
sheet of any "Assemble It Yourself" kit

"Blah blah blah flowers, blah blah blah protocol. Understood?"

"Uh huh," I said, looking out the window.

When I had agreed to hear the plans for the upcoming marriage between Massha and General Badaxe, I had done it without realizing how long it would take or how complex the ceremony would be. After several hours of this, however, I realized that my own part was going to be minimal, and was having a great deal of difficulty paying attention to the myriad of details.

"Of course, blah blah blah . . . "

And they were off again.

A bird landed on a branch outside the window and began gobbling down a worm. I found myself envying him. Not that I was particularly hungry, mind you. It was just that the way my life had been going lately, eating a worm seemed like a preferable alternative.

"Have you got that? Skeeve?"

I jerked my mind back to the task at hand, only to find my massive apprentice peering at me intently. Obviously, I had just missed something I was supposed to respond to.

"Umm . . . Not really, Massha. Could you summarize it again briefly so I can be sure I have it right?"

I didn't mean to emphasize the word 'briefly,' but she caught it anyway.

"Hmmm," she said, fixing me with a suspicious stare. "Maybe we should take a break for a few minutes," she said. "I think we could all do with a good stretch of the legs."

"If you say so, my dear," the General said, rising obediently to his feet.

I admired his stamina . . . and his patience. I was sure that this was as tedious for him as it was for me, but you'd never tell it to look at him.

I started to rise as well, then sank back quickly into my seat as a wave of dizziness hit me.

"Hey Skeeve! Are you all right?"

Massha was suddenly more concerned than she had been a moment before.

"I'm fine," I said, trying to focus my eyes.

"Would you like some wine?"

"*No!!* I mean, I'm all right. Really. I just didn't get much sleep last night is all."

"Uh huh. Out tom-catting again, were you, Hot Stuff?"

Normally, I kind of enjoyed Massha's banter. Today, though, I was just too tired to play.

"Actually, I went to bed fairly early," I said, stuffily. "I just had a lot of trouble getting to sleep. I guess there was just too much on my mind to relax."

That was a bit of an understatement. Actually, I had tossed and turned most of the night . . . just as I had for the two pervious nights. I had hoped that once I had dealt with the money problems I had been wrestling with, I could concentrate on making up my mind about whether or not to marry Queen Hemlock. Instead, all the factors and ramifications kept dancing in my head, jostling each other for importance, until I couldn't focus on any of them. Unfortunately, I couldn't put them aside, either.

"Uh huh," she said, peering at me carefully.

Whatever she saw, she didn't like. Pushing two chairs together, she sat down next to me a put a motherly hand on my shoulder.

"Come on, Skeeve," she said. "Tell Massha all about it. What is it that's eating you up lately?"

"It's this whole thing about whether or not to marry Queen Hemlock," I said. "I just can't seem to make up my mind. As near as I can tell, there isn't a clear cut right answer. Any option I have seems to be loaded with negatives. Whatever I do is going to affect so many people, I'm paralytic for fear of doing the wrong thing. I'm so afraid of doing something wrong, I'm not doing anything at all."

Massha heaved a great sigh.

"Well, I can't make that call for you, Skeeve. Nobody can. If it's any help, though, you should know that you're loved, and that your friends will standby whatever decision you reach. I know it's rough right now, but we have every faith that you'll do the right thing."

I guess that was supposed to be reassuring. It flashed across my mind, however, that I really didn't need to be reminded of how much everyone was counting on me to reach the right decision . . . when after weeks of deliberation I still didn't have the foggiest idea of what the right decision was! Still, my apprentice was trying to help the only way she knew how, and I didn't want to hurt her for that.

"Thanks, Massha," I said, forcing a smile. "That does help a bit."

"Ahem."

I glanced up to see General Badaxe stepping forward. He had been so quiet I had forgotten he was in the room until he cleared his voice.

"Will you excuse us, my dear? I'd like to have a word with Lord Skeeve."

Massha glanced back and forth between the General and me, then shrugged.

"Sure thing, Hugh. Gods know I've got enough to keep me busy for a while. Catch you later, Hot Shot."

The General closed the door behind her, then stood regarding me for several moments. Then he came over to where I was standing and placed both of his hands on my shoulders.

"Lord Skeeve," he said. "May I be permitted the privilege of speaking to you, of treating you for a few moments as if you were my own son . . . or a man under my command in the Army?"

"Certainly, General," I said, genuinely touched.

"Fine," he smiled. "Turn around."

"Excuse me?"

"I said 'Turn around.' Face in the other direction, if you will."

Puzzled, I turned my back on him and waited.

Suddenly, something slammed into my rear end, propelling me forward with such force that I nearly fell, saving myself only by catching my weight with my hands and one knee.

I was shocked.

Incredible as it seemed, I had every reason to believe the General had just kicked me in the rump!

"You kicked me!" I said, still not quite believing it.

"That's right," Badaxe said calmly. "Frankly, it's long overdue. I had considered hitting you over the head, but it seems that lately your brains are located at the other end."

Grudgingly, I began to believe it.

"But why?" I demanded.

"Because, Lord Skeeve, with all respect and courtesies due your station and rank, it is my studied opinion that you've been acting like the north end of a south-bound horse."

That was clear enough. Surprisingly poetic for a military man, but clear.

"Could you be a bit more specific?" I said, with as much dignity as I could muster.

"I'm referring to your possible marriage to Queen Hemlock, of course," he said. "Or, more specifically, your difficulty in

160

making up your mind. You're agonizing over the decision, when it's obvious to the most casual observer that you don't want to marry her."

"There are bigger issues at stake here than what I want, General," I said wearily.

"Bullshit," Badaxe said firmly.

"What?"

"I said 'Bullshit,'" the General repeated, "and I meant it. What you want is the only issue worth considering."

I found myself smiling in spite of my depression.

"Excuse me, General, but isn't that a little strange coming from you?

"How so?"

"Well, as a soldier, you've devoted your life to the rigors of training and combat. The whole military system is based on self sacrifice and self denial, isn't it?"

"Perhaps," Badaxe said. "Has it occurred to you, though, that it's simply a means to an end? The whole idea of being prepared for combat is to be able to defend or exert what *you* want against what someone else wants."

I sat up straight.

"I never thought of it that way."

"It's the only way *to* think of it," the General said, firmly. "Oh, I know a lot of people see a soldier's life as being subservient. That it's the role of a mindless robot subject to the nonsensical orders and whims of his superior officers . . . including Generals. The fact is that an army has to be united in purpose, or it's ineffectual. Each man in it *voluntarily* agrees to follow the chain of command because *it's the most effective way to achieve a common goal.* A soldier who doesn't know what he wants or why he's fighting is worthless. Even worse, he's a danger to anyone and everyone who's counting on him."

He paused, then shook his head.

"For the moment, however, let's consider this on a smaller scale. Think of a young man who trains himself so that he won't be bullied by older, larger men. He lifts weights to develop his muscles, studies various forms of armed and unarmed combat, and practices long hard hours with one objective in mind: To harden himself to where he won't *have* to knuckle under to anyone."

The General smiled.

"What would you say, then, if that same young man subsequently let every pipsqueak and bravo shove him around because he was afraid he'd hurt them if he pushed back?"

"I'd say he was a bloody idiot."

"Yes," Badaxe nodded. "You are."

"Me?"

"Certainly," the General said, starting to look a little vexed. "Didn't you recognize yourself in the picture I just described?"

"General," I said, wearily, "I haven't gotten much sleep for several days. now. Forgive me if I'm not tracking at my normal speed, but you're going to have to spell it out for me."

"Very well. I spoke about a young man building himself up physically. Well, you, my young friend, are probably the most formidable man I know."

"I am?"

"Beyond a doubt. What's more, like the young man in my example, you've built yourself up over the years . . . even in the time I've known you. With your magikal skills and wealth, not to mention your allies, supporters, and contacts, you don't have to do anything you don't want to. What's more, you've proved that time and time again against some very impressive opposition."

He smiled and laid a surprisingly gentle hand on my shoulder.

"And now you tell me that you have to marry Hemlock even though you don't want to? I don't believe it."

"Well, the option is that she abdicates and I'm stuck with being king," I said, bitterly. "I want that even less."

"Then don't do that, either," the General shrugged. "How is anyone going to force you to do *either* if you don't voluntarily go along with it? I know I wouldn't want the job."

His simple analysis gave me a thread of hope, but I was still reluctant to grab for it.

"But people are counting on me," I protested.

"People are counting on you to do what is right for *you*. " Badaxe said firmly. "Though it's hard for you to see, they're *assuming* that you'll do *what you want to do*. You should have listened more closely to what my bride to be was saying to you. If you *want* to marry Queen Hemlock, they'll support you by not standing in the way or giving you grief. Do you really think, though, that if you firmly state that you *want* to continue working with them, that they won't support that with as much or more enthusiasm? *That's* what Massha was trying to say, but I think she was saying it too gently for you to hear. Everyone's been too gentle with you. Since you don't seem to know what you want, they've been walking on eggshells around you to let you sort it out. In the meantime, you've been straining to hear what everyone else wants rather than simply relaxing and admitting what *you* want."

I couldn't suppress my smile.

"Well, General," I said, "if there's one thing no one could accuse you of, it would be of not treating me overly gently."

"It seemed appropriate."

"That wasn't a complaint," I laughed. I was feeling good now, and didn't bother trying to hide it. "It was admiration . . . and thanks."

I extended my hand. He gathered it into his own and we exchanged a single, brief shake that sealed a new level in our friendship.

"I take it that you've reached your decision then?" Badaxe said, cocking an eyebrow at me.

"Affirmative," I smiled. "And your guess as to what it is would be correct. Thank you, sir. I hope it goes without saying that I'd like to return the favor sometime, should the opportunity present itself."

"Hmmm . . . If you could, perhaps, show a little greater interest in the plans for the wedding," the General said. "Particularly if you could come up with a way to shorten the planning procedure?"

"I can shorten today's session," I said. "Give Massha my apologies, but I feel the need to meet with Queen Hemlock. Perhaps we can continue the session tomorrow."

"That isn't shortening the process," Badaxe scowled. "It's prolonging it."

"Sorry, General," I laughed, heading out the back door. "The only other suggestion I'd have is to convince her to elope. I'll hold the ladder for you."

Chapter Nineteen

"There must be fifty ways to leave your lover!"
P. Simon

My mind finally made up at last, I set out to give the news to Queen Hemlock. I mean, since she was waiting for a decision from me, it wouldn't be right to delay sharing it once it had been made. Right? The fact that if I waited too long, I might chicken out entirely had nothing to do with it. Right?

Suddenly, I was very aware of the absence of my bodyguards. When I had given them their assignment to distribute my unwanted cash, it had been under the assumption that I was in no particular danger while here at the palace.

Now, I wasn't so sure.

I had noticed back when we first met, when I was masquerading as King Rodrick, that Queen Hemlock had a nasty, perhaps even a murderous streak in her. There had been no evidence of it lately, but then again, I wasn't aware of her having received any bad news of a degree such as I was bringing her, either.

I shook my head and told myself I was being silly. At her worst, the Queen was not taken to open, unpremeditated violence. If it looked like she was taking the news badly, I could simply gather the crew and skip off to another dimension before she could get around to formulating a plan for revenge. There was absolutely no reason for me to need bodyguards to protect me from her. Right?

I was still trying to convince myself of this when I reached the Queen's chambers. The honor guard standing outside her door snapped to attention, and it was too late for a graceful retreat.

Moving with a casualness I didn't feel, I knocked on her door.

"Who is it?"

"It's Skeeve, your Majesty. I was wondering if I might speak to you if it's not inconvenient?"

There was a pause, long enough for me to get my hope up, and then the door opened.

"Lord Skeeve. This is a pleasant surprise. Please, come right in."

Queen Hemlock was dressed in a simple orange gown, which was a pleasant surprise. That she was dressed, that is, not the color of it. The first time she had entertained me in her quarters, she had been naked when she opened the door, and it had put me at an uncomfortable disadvantage for that conversation. This time around, I figured I was going to need all the advantages I could muster.

"Your Majesty," I said, entering the room. I looked about quickly as she was shutting the door, and, when she turned, gestured toward a chair. "Please, if you could take a seat?"

She raised a questioning eyebrow at me, but took the indicated seat without argument.

"What's this all about, Skeeve?" she said. "You look so solemn."

There was no way of stalling further, so I plunged in.

"I wanted to let you know that I've made my decision regarding marrying you," I said.

"And that is?"

"I . . . Your Majesty, I'm both honored and flattered that you would consider me worthy of being your consort. I had never dreamed that such a possibility existed, and, when it was sug-

166

gested, had to take time to examine the concept."

"And . . . " she urged.

I realized that no amount of sugar coating would change the basic content of my decision, so I simply went for it.

"My final conclusion," I said, "is that I'm not ready for marriage at this time . . . to you or anyone else. To try to pretend otherwise would be a vast disservice to that person . . . and to myself. Between my work and studies as a magician, and my desire to travel and visit other dimensions, I simply have no time or interest in settling down right now. If I did, I would doubtless end up resenting whoever or whatever had forced me to do so. As such, I fear I must decline your kind offer."

Having said it, I braced myself for her reaction.

"Okay," she said.

I waited for a moment for her to continue, but when she didn't, I felt compelled to.

"As to your abdicating the throne to me . . . Your Majesty, I beg you to reconsider. I have no qualifications or desire to be the ruler of a kingdom. At best, I'm a good advisor . . . and even that's only with the considerable help of my colleagues and friends. I fear that if I were to attempt to undertake such a responsibility, the kingdom would suffer badly . . . I know I would . . . and . . . and . . . "

My oration ground to a halt as I saw that she was laughing.

"Your Majesty? Excuse me. Did I say something funny?"

"Oh Skeeve," she gasped, coming up for air. "Did you really think . . . Of course I'm not going to give up the throne. Are you kidding? I *love* being Queen."

"You do? But you said . . . "

"Oh, I say *lots* of things," she said, waving a negligent hand. "One of the nice things about being royalty is that you get to decide for yourself which of the things you say are for real and which should be ignored."

To say the least, I was confused.

"Then why did you say that if you didn't intend to follow through?" I said. "And how about your marriage proposal?

Didn't you mean that, either?"

"Oh, I meant it all right," she smiled. "But I didn't really expect you to want to marry me. I mean, why should you? You've already got wealth and power *without* being tied down to a throne or a wife. Why should you want to stay here and play second banana to me when you could be off hopping around the world or wherever it is that you go as the one and only Great Skeeve? It would have been fabulous for me and the kingdom to have you tied into us permanently, but there weren't any real benefits for you. That's why I came up with that abdication thing."

"Abdication thing?" I echoed weakly.

"Sure. I knew you didn't want to be a king. If you had, you would have kept the throne back when Roddie had you pose as him. Anyway, I figured that if you didn't want it bad enough, it just might make a big enough threat to lure you into playing consort for me instead."

She made a little face.

"I know it was weak, but it was the only card I had to play. What else could I do? Threaten you? With what? Even if I managed to come up with something that would present a threat to you and that menagerie of yours, all you'd have to do is wave your hands and blink off to somewhere else. It simply wouldn't be worth the effort and expense to keep tracking you down . . . no offense. Going with the abdication thing, I at least had a *chance* of getting you to consider marrying me . . . and if nothing came of it, no harm done."

I thought of the days and nights I had been spending agonizing over my decision. Then I thought about throttling the Queen.

"No harm done," I agreed.

"So," she said, settling back in her chair, "that's that. No marriage, no abdication. At least we can still be friends, can't we?"

"Friends?" I blinked.

Even though I had met her some time back, I had never really thought of Queen Hemlock as a friend.

"Why not?" she shrugged. "If I can't have you as a consort, I'm willing to give it a try as a friend. From what I've seen, you're pretty loyal to your friends, and I'd like to have *some* tie to you."

"But why should that be important to you? You're a Queen, and the ruler of a fairly vast kingdom to boot."

Hemlock cocked her head at me curiously.

"You really don't know, do you Skeeve? You're quite a powerful man yourself, Skeeve. I'd much rather have you as an ally, to the kingdom and for myself, than as an enemy. If you check around, I think you'll find a lot of people who would."

That sounded remarkably like what Badaxe had pointed out to me earlier.

"Besides," the Queen added, "you're a nice guy, and I don't really have many friends. You know, people I can talk to as equals who aren't afraid of me? I think in the long run, we have more problems in common than you realize."

"Except I'm in a better position to still be able to do what I want," I finished thoughtfully.

"Don't rub it in," Hemlock said, wrinkling her nose. "Well, what do you say? Friends?"

"Friends," I smiled.

On an impulse, I took her hand and kissed it lightly, then stood holding it for a few moments.

"If I may, your Majesty, let me add my personal thanks to you for taking my refusal so well? Even if you more than half expected it, it still must have stung your pride a bit. It must have been tempting to make me squirm a little in return."

The Queen threw back her head and laughed again.

"It wouldn't be real smart of me to give you a rough time, now, would it?" she said. "As I said before, you can be a real help to the kingdom, Skeeve, even if it only means hiring you occasionally as an independent contractor. If I made you feel too bad about not marrying me, then you wouldn't ever want to see me or the kingdom again."

"I really don't know," I admitted. "The court of Possiltum gave me my first paying job as a magician. I'll probably always have a bit of a soft spot for it. Then, too, your majesty is not without charm as a woman."

That last bit sort of slipped out, but the Queen didn't seem to mind.

"Just not quite charming enough to settle down with, eh?" she smiled. "Well, let me know when you have some leisure time on your hands, and maybe we can explore some alternatives together."

That *really* took me aback.

"Ahh . . . certainly, your Majesty. In the meantime, however, I fear it's nearly time for my colleagues and I to take our leave of Possiltum. From what Grimble tells me, the kingdom is nearly back on solid financial footing, and there are pressing matters which require our attention elsewhere."

"Of course," she said, rising to her feet. "Go with my personal gratitude, as well as the fees you so richly deserve. I'll be in touch."

I was so uncomfortable about the reference to our fees, that I was nearly to the door before her last comment sank in.

"Umm . . . Your Majesty?" I said, turning back to her. "One more thing. Next time you need me, could you just write a note like everyone else instead of sending me a finger? It was a bit unnerving when it arrived."

"No problem," she said. "By the way, could I have the finger back? If nothing else I'd like to have the ring to remember Roddie by."

"I thought you had it," I frowned. "I haven't seen it since our conversation when I first got back here."

"Hmm . . . I wonder where it's gotten to. Oh well, I'll put the maids to work looking for it. If you happen to come across it in your things, be a dear and send it back to me?"

"Certainly, Your Majesty. Goodbye."

With that, I gave her my deepest bow and left.

Chapter Twenty

"Meanwhile, back at reality . . . "
G. Lucas

I felt as if a huge weight had been lifted from my back! For the first time since my return from Perv, I was in control of my own destiny!

No more wondering about what I should or shouldn't do about marrying Queen Hemlock for the good of the kingdom, or the good of the team . . . or the good of civilization, for that matter. Things were back in perspective! My future was mine to do with as I wished, without the pressure of trying to sort out what was best for others.

I found myself whistling to myself as I strode through the castle corridors, something I hadn't done in a long while, and had to fight the temptation to break into a jig.

As soon as that realization it, that I was resisting a temptation, I immediately did a little hop-skip.

I was through trying to judge everything I did on whether or not other people thought it was proper . . . or, more specifically, whether I *thought* other people would think it was proper. From now on, I was going to do what *I* wanted to do . . . and the rest of the world, or the dimensions at large, could just bloody well adapt!

With that decision, I threw in an extra high kick. It may not have been classic dance, but it felt good. Heck! *I* felt good. Better than I could ever remember feeling.

I became aware of a couple people staring at me from afar, and a few more craning their necks for a better look. Rather than feeling embarrassed or self-conscious, I waved at them gaily and continued my prancing.

I had to tell someone! Share my new-found happiness with my friends. They had all stood by me through the bad times. Now I wanted to be with them when I felt *good!*

I'd tell Bunny . . . no, Aahz! I'd tell Aahz first and *then* Bunny. My partner deserved to be the first to know.

"Hey Boss! Skeeve!"

I turned to see Nunzio beckoning me from the other end of the corridor. I was surprised to see him, and started to wave. Then it dawned on me that this was the first time he had ever called *me* to join *him* instead of the other way around. A feeling of alarm swept away my earlier euphoria.

"Come quick, Boss! It's important!"

My fears were confirmed. Something was wrong. Something was *very* wrong.

I hurried to join him, but he moved off down the corridor ahead of me, looking back from time to time to see if I was following.

"Wait for me, Nunzio!" I called.

"Hurry, Boss!" he replied, not slackening his pace.

I was starting to get a bit winded trying to catch up with him, but if anything he seemed to be increasing his speed. Then he ducked down a flight of stairs, and an idea came to me.

When I reached the stairs, instead of descending normally, I vaulted over the railing and used my magik to fly (which is really levitation in reverse) after him. This seemed to be a bit faster than running, and certainly a lot easier on the lungs, so I kept it up. I managed to catch my breath *and* catch up with my bodyguard just as we were emerging into the palace courtyard.

"What's this all about, Nunzio?" I said, slowing my speed

to match his pace.

Instead of answering, he pointed ahead.

There was a group of people gathered in the courtyard. Some were guards or other people I had seen around the palace, but there also seemed to be a batch of costumed characters with them. Then I saw Guido and Pookie in the group . . . and Aahz!

"Hey Aahz! What's happening?" I called.

At the sound of my voice, the whole group looked in my direction, then fell back slightly and . . .

And then I saw what they were gathered around.

"GLEEP!"

My pet dragon was lying on his side, showing no sign of his usual energy and life.

I don't recall landing . . . or of moving at all. I just remember crouching at my pet's side and gathering his head into my lap.

"What's wrong, fellah?" I said, but got no response. "Aahz? What's the matter with him?"

"Skeeve, I . . . " my partner began, but then I saw it.

Protruding from Gleep's side, just behind his leg, was an arrow!

At that moment, I felt my pet stir in my arms, weakly trying to raise his head.

"Take it easy, fellah," I said, trying to sound soothing.

Gleep's eyes found mine.

"Skeeve?" he said faintly, then went limp, his head falling back on my lap.

He had said my name! The first thing he had ever said other than the sound that had given him his name.

I carefully eased his head onto the ground and rose. I stood looking down at him for several moments, then raised my eyes to the surrounding crowd. I don't know what my expression was, but they all gave ground several steps as my gaze passed over them.

When I spoke, I tried to keep my voice soft and level, but it seemed to come from far away.

"All right." I said. "I want to know what's been going on here . . . and I want to know *now!!*"

173

Indeed, what has been going on while Skeeve was preoccupied? Here is an advance peek at the next MythAdventure!

SOMETHING M.Y.T.H. INC.

Robert Asprin
Prologue

Like wildfire, word spread throughout the land . . . from town to village, from peddlar to peasant . . . that their once idyllic kingdom was now under the control of a mighty magician who held the Queen in thrall.

Though it was customary for the common folk to pay little attention to who it was that ruled them, much less the antics and machinations of palace politics, this time it was different.

It was clear to even a casual observer that the magician dabbled in the Black Arts. He openly associated with and sought counsel from demons, who even now roamed the corridors of the palace. As further evidence of his other worldly nature and preferences, the magician kept a fierce dragon as a pet . . . a rarity that even the animal loving ecologists of the land found disquieting. For those who would scoff at the existence of magik and other supernatural powers, there were frightening rumors of another sort. It was said that the so-called magician was connected to the criminal underground, trading political influence for their assistance in keeping the populace under control.

Even considering all this, the people might have been willing to ignore the power shift, were it not for one thing . . . their taxes were being raised. While it was true that, even with the new increases, their taxes were barely half of what they had once been, the populace saw it as a grim foreboding of things to come. Once the magician succeeded in reversing the trend from lowering taxes to increasing them, it was asked, where would it stop?

Clearly, something would have to be done.

People who had never thought of themselves as heroes began to ponder and mutter, both singly and in groups, about ways to bring down the tyrant. Though they varied greatly in both skills and intelligence, the sheer volume of the plotters virtually insured the eventual downfall of the villain currently growing fat off the kingdom . . . the man they called Skeeve the Great.

About the Author and Illustrator

Born in 1946, Robert Lynn Asprin is a first generation American of Philippine-Irish descent. Raised in the university town of Ann Arbor, Michigan, he was exposed to a wide range of bookstores, museums, and cultures from an early age. Attending the University of Michigan and enlisting in the Army during the stormy and controversial Vietnam era of the sixties only served to enhance his awareness and appreciation of diversity, and working his way through the accounting department of a small subsidiary of the Xerox corporation for twelve years prior to becoming a full time writer provided the finishing touches to his unique view of the people around him.

Bob has two children, Annette and Daniel. His interests are many and varied, ranging from fencing and music to tropical fish and needlework.

His new science fiction humor series, the Phule novels, are also gathering a wide following, and have appeared on the *New York Times* bestseller list.

Robert Asprin is currently living in the French Quarter, New Orleans.

Phil Foglio is an accomplished artist, writer, cartoonist, and satirist. Graduating with a BFA in cartooning, he began his association with Science Fiction fandom, winning Fan Artist Hugos in 1977 and 1978. Early in his career, he produced the "What's New" comic strip for *Dragon* magazine, two *Buck Godot* graphic novels, and the comic adaptation of Robert Asprin's *Mythadventures*.

Recently, he has produced two miniseries for DC Comics, *Angel and the Ape* and *Stanley and His Monster*. Since then, Phil has started his own comic company, Palliard Press, with long-time friend Greg Ketter. He has been able to produce the *What's New Collection*, *XXXenophile*, a humorous, politically correct, SF and Fantasy Adult Comic, and has once again begun to chronicle the adventures of *Buck Godot: Zap Gun for Hire*.

Today, Phil and his wife Kaja live in Seattle.